W9-DCJ-040

The Backyard Tribe

. . . .

Also by Neil Shulman, M.D.:

Finally . . . I'm a Doctor

Doc Hollywood (What? Dead . . . Again?)

Better Health Care for Less

Understanding Growth Hormone

High Blood Pressure

. . . .

THE BACKYARD TRIBE

NEIL B. SHULMAN M.D.

St. Martin's Press   New York

Design by Basha Zapatka

LIBRARY OF CONGRESS CATALOGING-IN-PUBLICATION DATA
Shulman, Neil.
    The backyard tribe / Neil Shulman.
        p.   cm.
    ISBN 0-312-10513-4
    1. Africans—Travel—Alabama—Fiction.   2. Masai (African people)—Fiction.   3. Physicians—Alabama—Fiction.   I. Title.
PS3569.H774N68   1994
813'.54—dc20   93-40480

First Edition April 1994

10   9   8   7   6   5   4   3   2   1

DEDICATION

We are indebted to the Maasai people who have much to teach all peoples of the world. This book was written in the belief that true multicultural understanding is not possible until everyone is able to laugh with each other.

The book was inspired by my trip to Kenya, where I helped organize a health screening program, which contributed to the establishment of the Heart to Heart Program. Heart to Heart is a program providing urgently needed heart surgery in America for children from developing countries. A special thanks to the founder and leader of this effort, Dr. Herman Taylor, whose guidance and generosity have made this program happen. I'd like to recognize my friends Mrs. Earnestine Taylor, Dr. James Reed, Dr. Dallas Hall, Dr. Elijah Saunders, Ms. Alicia Georges, and Dr. Charles Curry as well as the community of health care providers, organizations, families, and individuals whose volunteerism contributed to this wonderful humanitarian endeavor.

Ten percent of the royalties from the sale of this hardback book will be contributed to the Maasai and the Heart to Heart Program.

ACKNOWLEDGMENTS

Thanks to Hal Jacobs for his collaboration on this book and the screenplay. Also, I'd like to recognize Alicia, Daniel, and Henry Jacobs for their support.

All names and characters in this tale are either invented or used fictitiously. The episodes are fictional although often inspired by real experiences. Unlike some other healers, to my knowledge the Maasai laibons do not treat dementia by burying their patients alive.

PROLOGUE

The young Maasai girl crouched in the smooth dirt near her mother's dung-plastered hut. She seemed to study her bare feet as she gasped for air. Nothing. In a strangled voice, she called her mother's name.

Loud voices and footsteps reverberated throughout the settlement in the plains below Mount Kilimanjaro. Her mother glanced up from the cooking fire inside the darkened hut, then hurried outside.

Kneeling beside her daughter, she held her breath. How could she breathe when her only child could not? They waited together, their eyes locked on each other's, neither daring to speak.

But the spell didn't pass like the others. When her daughter finally closed her eyes, the mother cried out with the pain of childbirth, the terror of absolute love.

The equatorial sun rose higher in the sky. The Maasai healer, the laibon, arrived. He berated the demons for afflicting someone as pure and beautiful as this child. Crushing a handful of aromatic leaves in his hand, he cupped them over her nose and mouth.

Her eyes fluttered open. She gazed at the faces of the elders, warriors, mothers, and children gathered over her. Her mother held her tightly in her arms and rocked her, singing:

· · · ·

Grow up, my precious one,
To be as slender as the grass
and tall and strong as Mt. Kilimanjaro.

Grow up to bring happiness
To your brothers and sisters.

Grow up to help your mother.

ONE

Exactly on schedule, the Lufthansa flight from Frankfurt, West Germany to Nairobi, Kenya, was cleared for landing at Jomo Kenyatta International Airport.

"All right, folks. It's almost game time! Remember, photo ops exist only for those who seize them!"

Gordon Sharpe, tour guide for Beating Around the Bush Safaris, stood beneath the flashing seat belt sign and inspected his group of Americans. White pith helmets emblazoned with the safari logo bobbled on their heads. They were dressed in his-and-hers khakis, with enough Nikons, Sonys, and Bushnells strapped around their necks to stock a small camera store.

Gordon felt relieved to be with American safari tourists again. The deeper they ventured into the bush, the less obsessed they became over rooting out new species, and the more passionate they became over finding ice cubes and soft toilet paper.

"You bloody well won't find a Big Mac in the bush," Gordon said. "But I guarantee you'll come eyeball to eyeball with the most powerful creatures on this planet we call Earth. That's right. The Big Five. Elephants. Lions. Leopards. Buffalo. And the horny rhinoceroses."

"The Big Six if you count Gordon's ego," Gail Payne whispered to her husband.

"Why don't you ask Gordon why giraffes didn't make the Big Five?" asked Bud.

"I believe you have to belong to the tour group to ask silly questions."

Dr. and Mrs. Payne sat in the last aisle behind the tour group. They were the only passengers in their section not outfitted like contestants on an old TV game show.

"Here. This is what we need." Gail stopped flipping through the magazine on her seat-back tray.

Bud put down his *AMA Journal* and read aloud, "A luxurious minivan that redefines the way you see the world." He turned to Gail. "What's wrong with the way we see the world through our '86 Volvo station wagon?"

"You try carpooling with Douglas, Lisa, and four of their closest hellions one week. Or better yet, try hauling a few cypresses home from the nursery. Or pick up a load of granite stepping stones from the quarry. Or recycle . . ."

Bud flipped back the cover of the magazine. "The *Backyard Magazine?*"

"Don't sneer. An editor called about including our yard in their Over the Neighbor's Fence section." Gail, an amateur landscaper, was well known in local gardening circles for her virtuoso backyard. "Besides, you can get some good ideas from these magazines."

"Ten Reasons Why You Need a New Minivan," Bud read out loud.

"I didn't see that," Gail said. She quickly scanned the cover, displaying a Cape Cod residence with a backyard of sand dunes and sea oats designed by a prestigious Boston firm.

"Where did you see that?"

"I didn't." Bud dodged her playful jab.

"You tease," said Gail. "Wait till I get you alone."

"I can't wait."

Gail saw her reflection in the window, laughing to herself. Through the clouds she caught a glimpse of Nairobi, a wide urban sprawl of modern office buildings, hotels, parks, and highways.

"Oh, Bud," she said wistfully. "Next year I want to go on a real

. . . .

vacation. Somewhere romantic. Just you and me—and a villa in the Italian lake district."

"I thought we both agreed that these rural clinics can be pretty romantic. I may be seeing patients during the day, but at night it's just you and me."

"It's wonderful that you still want to volunteer in these developing nations, but next year . . ."

"Remember Costa Rica last year? Mmm?" Bud raised an eyebrow.

Last year Bud had volunteered to practice at a rural mountain clinic in Costa Rica. They both agreed that the five days, actually the four steamy nights, were better than their honeymoon in Jamaica twelve years ago.

Bud continued. "How 'bout New Guinea three years ago? What about our first year—the Mississippi Delta?"

He put his arm around her and Gail leaned her head against his shoulder.

"Mmmm . . . We always manage to recharge our batteries on these trips, don't we?"

"Exactly," said Bud. "It's so easy to get distracted these days. We need these trips to get back to the basics."

"It's nice to hear you say that. Go on."

"I mean it. Where else do I get a chance to be alone with a patient without a bunch of bean-counting, paper-pushing administrators and adjusters breathing down my neck every time I order a precautionary lab test or X ray?"

"I was thinking of different batteries, doctor," she whispered. "Good old-fashioned privacy, remember? No children, no carpools, no emergency calls. And best of all . . ."

She glanced down at his waist. "No beeper."

Suddenly Gordon filled the aisle next to them. "Remember, this is the African bush—not some stateside African-theme park built around a corn-dog stand. In the bush, anything *can* and *will* happen. Be prepared. You'll only have one chance to get the photographic shot of a lifetime."

"If it moves, shoot it," shouted a retired electrician from Detroit.

. . . .

"With one exception," Gordon paused dramatically. "The Maasai."

"Never heard of it!" a Fort Lauderdale furrier shouted. "What's it look like?"

"The Maasai are a tribe—Africa's greatest herders and warriors. They live exactly as they did a thousand years ago. But, thanks to Beating Around the Bush Safaris, you'll be able to step back in time when we visit an authentic Maasai village."

"Bull manure," said the older man sitting across the aisle from Bud. "Real Maasai don't play Wild Kingdom for tourists."

While crossing the Atlantic, Bud had learned that his aislemate, Zach Tyler, was the former host of "The Uncle Zach Show," a morning children's show in Peoria, Illinois. Uncle Zach had snowy white hair, laugh wrinkles, and a reassuring, Santa-like heft. He had the confidence of a man who went up against "Captain Kangaroo" year after year, and won the ratings game in his local market every time.

Gail smiled at Zach across the aisle, then leaned back close against Bud. "Just wait until I get you alone."

Once inside Nairobi's modern airport terminal, Bud and Gail strolled behind the safari group, allowing a generous gap to widen between them and the tourist flying-wedge formation.

Into the gap shuffled Zach Tyler. Gail noticed that Bud was closely monitoring the older man's progress. That was Bud for you. He became intimate with other people's frailties in a way that never ceased to amaze her. Like most doctors' companions, she had learned never to take his complete, undivided attention for granted.

Once Gail had come across this classified in the personals section of the Atlanta newspaper:

> DWF, 35, beautiful, athletic, seeks WM, 35-45, loves outdoors and fine dining. No diseases. No doctors.

. . . .

Gail understood perfectly where the DWF was coming from. So did Bud. He had burst out laughing after finding the ad taped to the bathroom mirror.

At the baggage claim, they picked up their luggage. A few moments later, Bud stopped beside the overheated Zach. The problem was even more acute. The ex–kiddie show host couldn't carry his two suitcases for more than a step at a time.

"Let me give you a hand," said Bud, reaching for a suitcase. "Are you feeling all right?"

"Yes, thanks." Zach mopped his forehead with a handkerchief. "Don't know how I got everything into two suitcases."

"It wasn't easy for us, either," Gail said reassuringly. The airline had strict luggage requirements: two pieces maximum, forty-four pounds apiece. Gail had organized each of their suitcases with the help of the bathroom scales.

Bud lifted the suitcase a few inches off the ground. Then immediately lowered it. The weight was closer to 144 pounds than the 44 required by the airlines.

Zach's warning look silenced him. "Kindly return it before we reach customs," he said.

Bud walked on, the suitcase knocking against his leg. Out of the corner of his mouth, he whispered to Gail, "I think he's got a corpse in here."

"Really?" Her eyes grew as wide as his.

"A fat corpse."

At customs, the officials were in excellent spirits. They nodded and waved the American safari group through without a second thought. There was a special place in their hearts for Americans wearing pith helmets.

Bud said nothing after he slid the suitcase back to Zach. Not only was it none of his business, they were downwind from customs. The officials could sniff out travelers' anxiety from fifty feet.

Gail smoothed down Bud's curly, tousled hair. After twelve years of marriage, she had finally begun to appreciate his unruly hair.

· · · ·

Whereas everything else in their lives had a predictable shape and feel, Bud's rogue hair defied every pair of scissors known to man.

Zach's turn. He managed to heave his suitcases the final ten feet to the customs counter. A few snowy white curls shook loose out of his pith helmet and fell down his reddening forehead.

"Do you have anything to declare?"

"No." Zach's arms were numb, his chest pounding. Long months of careful planning, including the charade of joining this safari group, all came down to this one moment. If the officials opened his suitcases, the result would be pandemonium.

The customs official scrutinized Zach's scarlet face. After a long pause, he waved him through, warning him to avoid overexposure to the equatorial sun.

Bud sighed with relief as he watched Zach stagger away with his suitcases.

"Do you have anything to declare?" the official asked Bud.

"No, sir."

"Please open your suitcase."

"Excuse me?"

"Please."

"Let me explain . . ."

An older official sauntered over to his colleague's side. He stared at the un-pith-helmeted Bud as if he expected trouble.

"Any problem?" he asked his partner.

"I don't think so."

Bud lifted his suitcase onto the counter, flicked both metal latches, then slowly lifted back the top.

The young official whistled. He stared into a suitcase containing the largest collection of pills, powders, vials, and hypodermics he'd ever stumbled across. Who knew the street value!

Bud began to reach into his inside jacket pocket. "I have a letter of authorization —"

"Stop. Keep your hands where I can see them!"

Bud raised his hands in the air. "It's okay. I'm a doctor. I was told I could bring in prescription drugs that were in short supply." He

. . . .

pointed at the bottles. "Penicillin, ampicillin, nitroglycerine . . ." He quickly reeled off a few more names.

"Step this way, please." The young customs official pointed towards a private room.

Bud's mind flashed ahead to the grueling interrogation scene under bright lights, the drugs scattered on the table in front of him, while he sweated in his T-shirt, repeating again and again, "I'm a family physician, I'm a family physician, a family . . ."

The older official said in a tired voice, "You say you're a doctor?" He held up a pill bottle. "What do we have here?"

"Pyridium."

"What's it prescribed for?"

"Pyridium is for simple bladder infection." Bud felt like a first-year resident being interrogated by the attending physician. "It stops bladder spasms and painful burning."

"Any side effects?"

"Nothing serious. It turns the urine red, that's all."

The official turned to his colleague. "That's right. My prescription ran out last month." He closed his hand over the Pyridium bottle.

"I'll keep this as evidence."

During the scene at customs, Gail had kept quiet. She knew that a simple phone call to the Kilbezi Clinic would have cleared up any misunderstanding over Bud's drug running. She also knew what the Auxiliary members would say when they heard about this one. The other hospital Auxiliary couples traveled first-class, slept in luxury hotels, and shopped in well-lit pedestrian malls. Their "close calls" usually involved a non-English-speaking salesclerk in a Paris boutique.

As they turned the corner toward ground transportation, she saw Zach Tyler waiting for them. She realized how much she enjoyed traveling off the beaten path and meeting characters like Zach.

"Thank you from the bottom of my heart," Zach said. "The heart was willing, but the biceps were weak." He rubbed his aching arms.

"Where's the tour group?" Gail saw no signs of the safari.

· · · ·

"Who cares?" said Zach, removing his pith helmet and sailing it toward a nearby trash can. "That was just to get through customs."

"Do we want to know what's in your luggage?" Bud asked.

"Do you, Dr. Payne?"

"Do we, Gail?"

"Sure."

"Communications equipment," Zach whispered. "Camcorders and battery packs, animation and graphics software, an editing board, and a miniature satellite disk—the keys to the global village."

"Marshall McLuhan's global village?" asked Gail, referring to the media scholar who had coined the expression in the mid-sixties.

"No," he said, smiling mysteriously. "Zach Tyler's global village."

A young nun, dressed in traditional habit and wimple, stood in the middle of the terminal corridor. She held up a piece of paper with DR. PAYNE written in block letters.

Sunlight flooded in the windows behind her as Bud and Gail approached.

"Good afternoon, Sister." Bud offered his hand. "I'm Dr. Payne. This is my wife, Gail."

"I'm Sister Beth." The rail-thin, dark-eyed nun stepped back, holding up two grease-stained hands. "The water pump went out on me in the Ngong Valley. That's why I'm late."

"You're not late," Gail reassured her. "We just landed."

"Don't worry." Sister Beth put on her calfskin driving gloves. "I'll make up for it on the drive back."

Bud and Gail followed her outside the terminal to the clinic's ancient, two-toned Plymouth. They had a few minutes to look around as she slowly revved the engine. Along the curb, cabbies smoked cigarettes and joked with one another. Gail was impressed by how crisp the sunshine in this high altitude felt. No wonder, she thought, that the British were in such a hurry to confiscate this uplands territory from the native Africans less than a hundred years ago.

Behind the Plymouth, the Beating Around the Bush group fin-

· · · ·

ished boarding their bus. As Gordon stood outside the bus door, he counted off each person entering the bus.

"Twenty-seven, twenty-eight, twenty-nine . . ." Gordon stared incredulously at his fellow guides, two young Kenyan men wearing pith helmets. "I'm missing a head."

Gail saw Zach at the same moment Gordon did. He was driving by in a battered-looking Land Rover. His suitcases were stacked neatly in the back.

"Thirty!" shouted Gordon, pointing Zach out to his guides. "Where the hell is Thirty going?"

A second later, Sister Beth clicked the stopwatch on the dial of her black diver's wristwatch. Bud and Gail barely had time to dig their fingers into the backseat vinyl, when the Plymouth peeled off, laying rubber for a hundred feet.

Downtown Nairobi was mostly a blur as Sister Beth whipped around corners, nailed straightaways, and flew over potholes. Bud and Gail bounced and swayed together in the middle of the roomy backseat. It didn't take long to realize that the good sister's reflexes were perfectly matched to the car and blacktop.

They drove past rolling grasslands that gave way to deep green fields of tea plants. Sister picked up more speed over the Ngong Hills, accelerating down into the Rift Valley. Giraffes loped freely across a dusty landscape dotted with umbrella-shaped acacia trees. Immense clouds drifted overhead, casting their shadows over the sparse land.

Bud put his arm around Gail. The backseat was getting warmer with each additional bounce and sway. She moved over closer to him and her eyes traveled down to his waist—no beeper. He really was all hers.

. . . .

TWO

The Kilbezi Clinic was set off the rural highway in a little oasis of shrubs and pebbled walkways. Sister Beth eased into the tarmac lot and parked in front of a small, tin-roofed cottage.

"Lord help me," Sister Beth said to herself as she punched her wristwatch. "Two and a half minutes off my best time."

She pointed at the cottage. "That's for tourist doctors . . . I mean, guest doctors. Make yourselves at home."

"Thanks," said Gail. She tightened her grip on Bud's hand. "I guess we'll go inside and freshen up first."

"Tell everyone we'll be right out," added Bud.

They stepped out of the car, grabbed their suitcases, and ran toward the cottage door. Gail stopped with her hand on the doorknob. A loud noise roared close overhead.

Shielding their eyes from the sun, they watched the small airplane suddenly drop out of the sky toward them.

"It's the flying doctor," Sister Beth called out to them.

"Really?" Bud asked, starstruck. He explained to Gail. "Flying doctors service the outlying areas that can't be reached by car or boat. You might say they're the Indian Joneses of family physicians."

The tires of the rusting, battered little Cessna touched down on the tarmac as the flying doctor taxied toward them. Immediately, orderlies rushed out of the clinic carrying boxes of plasma, IVs, and sheets, and began loading the plane.

· · · ·

The flying doctor stepped down from the plane. She snugged her oil-stained Reds baseball cap over what used to be flaming red hair. She leaned heavily to her left as she walked toward Bud. Her face was grim, as no-nonsense as her blue workshirt, heavy corduroy pants, and laced-up black leather boots.

"You must be the new tourist doctor," she said to Bud.

Sister Beth murmured a hasty introduction. "Dr. Bernard Payne and Mrs. Gail Payne, this is Dr. Elizabeth Handy."

"Liz." She held out her heavily calloused hand.

"Bud." They shook hands.

"Well, Budweiser. You came just in time. I could use a good pair of hands. We've got a young man out there who became a scratching post for a lion."

"He was attacked by a lion?"

Liz winked good-humoredly at Sister Beth. "I believe it was the other way around. He's a Maasai warrior. Or was, if we don't boogie."

"We?" asked Gail.

"That's right. He can't be more than sixty kilometers east." She took off her bifocals, pulled out her torn shirttail, and began vigorously rubbing. "There're no roads in or out. We'll be lucky to land on a slick cow paddy."

"Excuse me," Gail said. "You said *we?*"

"Yes, ma'am. Loosely speaking. Actually there's just room for me and Budweiser here." Liz added with a big grin, "I guess this Bud's for me."

Bud turned to Sister Beth. "Doesn't the clinic have another doctor on call?"

"We do." Sister Beth jangled the car keys in her pocket. *"She's* on a call right now."

Standing beside the airplane, the orderlies slammed the cargo door shut. The plane shook and creaked, then a bolt rattled onto the parking lot.

"Not so rough!" Liz shouted. "How'd you like me to slap *you* around like that?"

. . . .

The men grinned and shook their heads as they returned to the clinic.

"Well, Doctor, looks like we're cleared for takeoff," said Liz.

"Excuse me," said Bud. "After a sixteen-hour international flight and Sister Beth's qualifying run from the airport, I don't think I'm in any condition to perform emergency surgery."

"Better get your medical bag," said Liz, walking stiffly back to the plane.

Bud faced Gail. "This should only take a couple of hours," he said stoically.

A few minutes later, as they kissed good-bye, Bud whispered, "Tomorrow morning, I don't care what anybody says. We're sleeping in."

THREE

Zach Tyler drove the Land Rover up the steep washed-out dirt road that ascended Mount Olerumbe. It was one year earlier that he had journeyed here for the first time. Armed with a rented jeep, a topographical map, and two heavy suitcases, he had met the Maasai people.

Zach had prepared his first words to the elders in Swahili. "Africa is the birthplace of man. This is where humans first learned to dance. And this is where they will learn to live in harmony."

The Maasai elders listened politely. Years ago, the oloiboni, a priest/prophet/soothsayer, had predicted the arrival of a man with hair like soapstone and eyes the color of the blue sky, who would bring the voice of millions with him.

Of course, the elders didn't bother to tell Zach this. They politely listened to his opening statement.

"If you share your ancient home with me," Zach said, "I'll share my modern tools with you. Together we will build a global village."

In the late 1940s, Zach was one of those who saw the tremendous potential of television. Thus the "Uncle Zach Show" was born in the midsize Peoria market. Children and mothers loved him. Over the course of thirty years, thousands of children strove heroically "for grades, mother, and country" and the chance of getting a seat for the show. But Zach had set his sights on building a new family. A global family. The year before the safari, after much intensive research, he had hit upon the seminomadic Maasai people of Kenya and neighboring Tanzania. The Maasai were proud, strong, culturally advanced, family-oriented, and exceedingly photogenic.

Before flying to Kenya the first time, he had sat down at a conference table with two creative executives from the Global News Network (GNN) in Atlanta. Zach had pitched "The Maasai Minute," a sixty-second segment dealing with the day-to-day subtleties of a native culture living in complete harmony with the environment. The young executives sipped cans of Coca-Cola and listened politely as Zach laid out his plan to smuggle high-tech video equipment into Kenya so that Maasai warriors could produce "The Maasai Minute" entirely on their own. Afterward, they told Zach that he should feel free to pitch the idea to other networks and producers in case they were slow in getting back to him.

In Kenya the Maasai elders were also fairly noncommittal as they shooed flies away with their wildebeest-tail fly whisks and listened to Zach's offbeat proposal. Finally, Loomo, an enterprising junior elder in his late thirties, took responsibility for Zach. "It could be worse," said Loomo. "He could be a missionary."

So, Zach had left Loomo precise instructions on how to maintain his modern tools: solar energy panels, videocassette player, and large-screen monitor. Meanwhile, Zach returned to the U.S. to pick up more communications equipment. Electronic goodies such as camcorders, rechargeable batteries, editing equipment, and a miniature satellite dish that could link the Maasai village with other global villages such as New York, Tokyo, and Berlin.

Zach was still an hour's drive from the global village when Loomo opened the Village Walk-In box office. Tonight's twin bill featured *Psycho* and *The Ten Commandments*. The Maasai were both tribal- and family-oriented. That's why Loomo thought the two stories, one about a mother and son who operate an inn, and the other about a tribe wandering in the desert, would play well together.

Elders from all over the district huddled near the sacred fig tree to catch up on each other's business. Women herded their children

· · · ·

and goats, greeting each other with laughter and embraces. Ankle bells tinkled as warriors filed in together, showing off their fine physiques and long coiffed hair in front of admiring young girls who wore their finest beaded necklaces, earrings, and tiaras on their shaved heads.

Loomo had gotten into show business the way most people do. By knowing the right people. There he was. Minding his own beeswax. His life was simple. Eleven children, two wives, and a herd of fine cattle. Then he met Zach Tyler. On his first visit, Zach had shown Loomo the path to fame and fortune by leaving behind solar panels, monitor, VCR, and two videocassettes: *What Immunization Means to You* and *What a Proper Diet Means to You*. Actually three tapes. Loomo had discovered the third tape stuffed in an old equipment bag after Zach's departure. *Black Emmanuel in Bangkok* had proved to be a lot more popular with Loomo's audience than the other two titles.

A simple man would've watched *Black Emmanuel* until the video-tape wore out and never thought anything more about it. But Loomo was not a simple man. He noted a name and address on the back of the tape. With the assistance of his youngest son, he wrote the following letter.

> Dear Flockbuster,
> My name is Loomo. You do not know me. I am Maasai elder. Once I help the whites when I kill a lion that ate three Germans and a baby. Now you can help me. Please send more movies.
> Honorably Yours, Loomo

The letter, once its authenticity was checked out, was a great hit at the home office of the world's largest videocassette retailer. Not even Madison Avenue could have dreamed up a better ad campaign. Immediately a video crew rushed out to document the delivery of 1,400 used videotapes to the remote East African village.

Later, a cooler head in the board room was said to have protested: "Folks, seriously now, how would you like to be on an African tent

· · · ·

safari with your family while nearby warriors watch *Slumber Party Massacre 3?*" But Loomo had already received his 1,400 titles in three large wooden crates. He still played *Immunization* and *Proper Diet* before every show. Why? Partly out of respect to Zach. Mostly because the tapes helped to settle down his audience before the main feature.

Loomo stopped by the box office. Tonight's take wasn't bad. Three shillings, one hen's egg, one beaded bracelet, a piece of honeycomb, and one damp sugar packet from the Nairobi Intercontinental Hotel. And it was still early. Maasai families pushed together and filled up the good sections up front near the video monitor. They settled down on grass mats and made themselves comfortable. Loomo glanced nervously at the concessions. Business was brisk. Farther down the line, he saw two missionaries waiting to enter. He waved hello. Missionaries always paid in shillings.

It was just getting dark when Zach Tyler drove the final hundred yards to the global village. He was arriving a few days early. He couldn't wait to see their surprised faces as they queued up to greet him.

He hesitated behind the Land Rover. Loud screeching sounds were coming from the village. At first it sounded like an exotic flock of birds. Then he started walking faster. Now he remembered where he had heard that sound before. Those weren't birds. Those were violins! Hitchcock's violins from the shower scene in *Psycho!* Since when did inhabitants of the global village watch Hitchcock?

The Maasai waited breathlessly as the woman stepped into the hot shower. Even in Nairobi, water pressure wasn't that good! The knife that suddenly flashed into view didn't surprise them in the least. After seeing all the *Halloween* movies and hundreds of other slasher films, the Maasai were surprised only when nubile young women *weren't* slashed to death.

"Ahhh!" Zach raced toward the crowd of moviegoers waving his arms over his head. "I came here to enlighten, not frighten!"

Loomo's fierce warrior-bouncers stepped out of the shadows toward him.

. . . .

"Where's Loomo?" Zach roared like a wounded lion.

"Shhhh . . ." said the audience.

Even as the warriors raised their spears to silence him, they kept one eye on the screen. Blood swirled down the bathtub drain. The suspense was awful. Where did all that water go after it poured down the hole?

Loomo poked his head out of his office. Across his desk lay beads, eggs, cuts of meat, loose cigarettes, sugar packets, shillings, feathers, and unidentifiable grayish matter. A good night at the box office.

"Zach Tyler!"

"Psycho?" Zach's face was red as a beet. *"Psycho,* Loomo?"

"Yes . . . Big hit. *Psycho* is very big hit!"

Zach closed his eyes and quickly counted three Mississippis. "No big hit." He shook his white hair. "Cruel and twisted. Bad. Very bad."

"I can't explain it, Zach." Loomo shrugged helplessly. "But it works for me." In Swahili he could have discussed the pros and cons of *Psycho* all night. But his English was limited to whatever he could pick up from Flockbuster videos.

"Let's turn it off. We're wasting solar energy."

"Sorry, Zach. No can do."

"Don't you see what you're doing? You're commercializing the global village!"

"Shhhhh . . ." An elder put his finger to his lips and stared pointedly at Zach.

Loomo rested his arm around Zach's shoulders. "C'mon into my office, Zach. Let's do tea and talk about this global village thing."

FOUR

The moment Bud saw Kimo, the wounded Maasai warrior, he knew they wouldn't be moving him anytime soon. Fever and infection were ravaging his body. He'd been losing ground ever since the lion ran over him.

Bud's experiences with treating animal-related injuries was limited to dogs, cats, and the odd, disgruntled squirrel. This was his first, and hopefully his last, lion mauling.

The lion's claws had slashed open the warrior's chest, raking downward to the groin. Much worse, however, was that the claws were carrying a cargo of toxins—hair and dirt and fecal material—which were now deeply embedded in Kimo's lacerated body. Fortunately, the major organs were intact.

"From what his people have told me, it's not the first time he's carried the mouth spike." Liz pointed at the old, ridged scars from a previous attack.

"The mouth spike?"

Liz described the ritual of the lion hunt as she aimed the flashlight, and Bud probed the inflamed tissue with surgical precision, cleaning and stitching usable tissue together.

"When the warriors surround the lion at the end of the long chase, they're armed with their long-bladed spears, buffalo-hide shields, and raw Maasai courage. All except one."

She pointed at the warrior stretched out before them. "Instead of a spear, our lion matador held the carved-out handle of a mouth spike. It's a hand-size bone sharpened at both ends.

"When the lion lunged toward him, he held his ground. He waited until he felt the lion's hot breath on his, then he rammed the spike inside the lion's mouth. Then he was plowed open."

Six hours ago the doctors had stepped into the twilight darkness of the dung-plastered hut. The smoky air clung heavily to the walls, pungent with the smells of livestock, sour milk, and putrefying wounds. With supplies from the plane, they had transformed the hut into a makeshift emergency room. As they continued to clean and stitch, Kimo rested quietly on sterile sheets. He was injected with 50ml of morphine every three hours. A catheter inserted in his forearm led to a bag of Ringer's solution that Liz had strung from an exposed branch in the hut's ceiling. Portable oxygen was close by.

The hut was becoming exceedingly crowded with Maasai elders, a polite, dignified group of older men. They solemnly observed Bud and Liz's surgical procedures, discussing matters in low, throaty voices. With heavy, dusty blankets draped around their bodies, they reminded Bud of a group of statesmen from ancient Rome. Then a late arrival abruptly shouldered his way in between Bud and Liz. He resembled the other elders, but he wore a leather pouch around his neck, carried a baton carved from a rhino horn, and displayed a fiery temper. He raised his voice, gesturing angrily with the shiny baton.

"What's his problem?" Bud said quietly, without glancing up, as he slid his index finger inside some crusty tissue below the rib cage.

"He's the laibon," Liz said. "A combination of doctor, priest, and teacher." She listened carefully, then added, "He says we should leave Kimo to the spirits. Our medicine cannot help. This is God's way."

"Ask him to move back," said Bud.

Rattling noises in the corner of the hut caught their attention.

"Just a minute," said Liz.

She peered into the darkness to watch the laibon and elders gathered around an older, highly distinguished elder. He sat on the

· · · ·

ground, shaking a cow horn, then carefully poured the stones out on the dirt. His hands felt the layout of the pebbles.

"What is this?" asked Bud. "The game room?"

"Shhh . . . That gentleman is the oloiboni, a revered holy man. He's asking God if we should leave."

Murmuring softly to the elders, the oloiboni stared in the direction of Bud and Liz. One by one, the Maasai followed the direction of his gaze.

"No way," Bud said to the elders. "We're not leaving. Kimo doesn't have a chance without us."

"It's okay." Liz sighed. "We can stay. The oloiboni says God sent us here for a reason."

Bud watched the elders gather their robes around their tall, stooping bodies and leave the hut. The laibon went last, glaring defiantly at Bud.

"What would you do if he said we had to leave?" Bud asked Liz.

She didn't hesitate. "The more I'm around these people, the more I respect their choices."

Bud took a deep breath, then stared down at the flashlight trail cast across Kimo's wounds. He didn't want to know what time it was. Clock watching and emergency surgery didn't go well together.

Occasionally his mind drifted over his lightheadedness, or stiffening back, or his sandpapery eyes. And worse—the incredible disappointment that swirled through his chest every time he thought of Gail alone at the clinic.

The tambourine shaking in the hands of Sister Lucille seemed to enjoy a life of its own. A dozen other sisters sat around the worn sofas in the music room and jammed with bongos, ukuleles, cymbals, clackers, and other folk instruments. Gail, sandwiched between Sister Xavier and Boniface swaying back and forth on a sunken couch, had never realized there were so many Swahili folk songs. The end of the song caught her by surprise. She clapped her hand over an Olympic-size yawn. Every eye in the room focused on her.

"You must be exhausted," said Sister Lucille. She glanced at a

· · · ·

much older nun, who smiled guiltily. "I'm afraid we got carried away with that last number."

"Perhaps I should call it a night," said Gail. With the help of her seatmates, she got to her feet.

"Sister Jill, if you hear anything . . ."

Sister Jill wiped her mouth harp on the hem of her robe. "Mrs. Payne, if anything comes over the radio, we'll let you know."

Outside the clinic, Gail felt wide awake again. The evening air was cool. The sky was brilliant with stars. She held her breath, praying for the little Cessna to swoop down and land in front of her.

Nothing happened.

The lights were off inside the guest cottage. Farther down the parking lot, country music drifted out of a brightly lit shed.

Gail realized she wasn't ready to face her first night in Kenya alone. She walked toward the light.

The Plymouth was parked inside the corrugated carport. On the shed's walls, someone had gone to the trouble of painting yellow outlines around the various tools. A bold-lettered sign said, "Neither a borrower nor a lender be. This garage does not loan out tools. That means you. Sister Beth."

Sister Beth was lying on a roller half under the car.

"Hi," said Gail.

Thump. Sister Beth's head slammed against the car's oil pan.

"I'm sorry. I saw the light on."

Sister Beth slid out on rollers. She slowly sat up, rubbed her oil-smeared forehead, then stared at the oil wrench in her hand as if she was unsure of its purpose.

"Looks like Bud and the flying doctor are going to be out there all night," said Gail, wandering around the car. "Sister Lucille says it's too risky to take off after dark."

Gail lightly touched a crescent wrench hanging on the wall. It fell, knocking over a jar of washers on the way down. The washers rolled crazily to all corners of the garage.

"I'm so sorry. I'll get them." She got down on her hands and knees and began picking up washers. "I guess those landings and takeoffs can be pretty hairy in the bush. And a lion attack must be horrible.

· · · ·

23

Sister Jill said they probably haven't been able to leave the man's side long enough to radio in."

Gail crawled to the end of the garage. A few feet from the car bumper, she saw row after row of flowering violets in ceramic pots.

"Oh, my . . . These violets are stunning. Of course, they're African violets." She turned around to face Sister Beth. "You like flowers?"

"I love flowers."

"So do I. My backyard is full of them."

"You like cars?" Sister Beth fixed Gail with a searchlight stare. Evidently she needed a friend as desperately as Gail did.

Gail squared her shoulders. "I love cars."

Bud sat leaning against the wall of the dung-plastered hut. He had no idea what time it was when he registered a change in Kimo's breathing. Getting to his feet, he snapped on the flashlight. Liz was gone.

Kimo's eyes were wide open, extremely bloodshot, the pupils dark and dilated.

"Thanks awfully much, Doctor," Kimo said with a heavy English accent.

A cold chill ran down Bud's spine. He had once read a journal article about doctors who dreamed they could communicate with comatose patients. Afterward, the doctors said they approached their patients with renewed vigor. Bud had never experienced anything like that until now. It was nice. Kimo's voice sounded a lot like Cary Grant's.

"How do you feel?" Bud asked.

"Like I was run over by a bloody lion."

"Where did you learn to speak English?"

"In London. Drove a taxicab out of Heathrow for three years."

"I had a layover in Heathrow once."

"Really?"

Bud could tell the warrior was just being polite.

"What are you doing here?" Kimo asked calmly.

"I'm with the flying doctor."

. . . .

"The Flying Lizard?" Kimo tried to smile, but a small groan escaped his lips instead. "English gives me such a bleeding headache."

"Then no more English for you." Bud placed his hand on Kimo's forehead. "You need to save your energy."

Liz stepped inside the hut and stared uncertainly at Bud.

"Who are you talking to?"

"Did you hear us?"

"Who?"

"Me and Kimo?" Bud could hardly believe it himself. "He speaks perfect English."

"Why don't you go out and get some fresh air?"

"You don't believe me? He told me he drove a cab out of Heathrow Airport."

"Sometimes these dung-plastered walls are filled with mushroom spores." She reached over and patted Bud's shoulder.

"He called you the Flying Lizard."

"Get some shut-eye, Budweiser," Liz said sharply. "We've got a long day ahead of us."

Bud drifted asleep to the sounds of warriors singing in rapid falsetto accompanied by a bass chorus. Then the women would take over the singing, challenging the warriors to reply. Their bare feet shuffled and scraped along the smooth dirt clearing inside the thorn fence.

· · · ·

FIVE

The sun rising over the Maasai settlement in the African plains was a dramatic sight. Seven dung-plastered huts encircled by a thorn fence blended intimately into the tawny plains. In the distance, Mount Kilimanjaro loomed over the ancient Maasai pasturelands.

The serenity of this pastoral scene—man living in harmony with nature—was worthy of a *National Geographic* photo spread. In fact, Bud wished he was back home, stretched out in his bed, with a copy of that *National Geographic* close by on his nightstand. As he staggered to the entrance of the intensive-care dung hut and stared out through bloodshot eyes, every cell in his body cried out for coffee. He tried to stretch his arms, but gave up after a few painful moments.

In the village center, an elder wrapped tightly in his blanket stooped down beside a urinating bull and held his cattle stick in the yellow stream. Another elder hurried over to join him so that he could receive his share of good luck that day. All Bud could think of were those hot-drink vending machines in every waiting room in the hospital that churned out the sorriest coffee in the world. What he wouldn't give for one this morning.

Then he saw her. A young girl, perhaps ten or eleven years old, leading her goats through the settlement. He heard the sound of her beaded necklaces clicking softly together as she nodded to the elders beside the bull.

Even in his exhausted condition, perhaps owing to it, Bud felt overwhelmed by the child's radiance. She was the princess of every fairy tale he'd ever read to his children—a vision of grace, beauty, and innocence. Her eyes had a startling clarity. Her neck, chest, and arms were adorned with beaded necklaces befitting a princess. Her head was shaved like all the women's, but she wore a special beaded tiara that set her apart.

Bud smiled at her. As she came closer, she stopped to greet him. Her smile was unforgettable. The smile alone was enough to make Bud feel lucky for being there.

Then Bud noticed something else. Her rasping, labored breathing. He took out his stethoscope and after a moment of pantomiming to get permission, he knelt down and listened to her chest.

"Rheumatic heart disease," said Liz. She watched him from the entrance to Kimo's hut.

"What can we do?" Bud took the stethoscope from around his neck and handed it to the girl to inspect. He never saw cases of rheumatic heart disease in the States. Antibiotics had virtually wiped it out in the Western world.

"There're forty thousand and children in this country with rheumatic heart disease like hers." Liz let this sink in. "In Nairobi there're two pediatric cardiologists, one cardiac surgeon, one heart-lung machine, and a three-year waiting list for pediatric surgery."

"If I was in the States, I could call one number to get help." Back home he could schedule his patients on a trip to the moon as long as their medical insurance covered it.

"It's like a sinking ship here," said Liz. "What we really need is penicillin to plug the hole. If we can treat strep throat, and prevent rheumatic heart disease, we might be able to stay afloat. But these days, even the bucket we're bailing with has a hole in it."

Liz saw Bud's concern. "You want to help? Send me penicillin."

"But that won't help her."

"I can save a hundred children before they get to her stage of disease."

· · · ·

27

Before Bud could reply, warriors walked past them herding cows. Women, elders, and children rushed from their huts laughing and pointing.

Liz seemed grateful for the distraction.

"The warriors are coming back from a cattle raid," she explained. "The Maasai believe that in the beginning of time, God gave all the cows on earth to them. Now, if they see a cow they want, they just take it." She chuckled to herself. "They figure it must be one of theirs that wandered away."

Bud removed his pen from his shirt pocket and handed it to the girl.

"Coca-Cola," she said, beaming proudly.

"Ah, Coca-Cola," said Bud. "You speak Coca-Cola?"

"Coca-Cola." She took the stethoscope from around her neck and handed it back to him.

Liz continued. "The Maasai value cows over almost everything," she said. "Except their children."

The Plymouth tore down the dirt two-lane, leaving a cloud of dust in its wake. Gail gripped the steering wheel, listening carefully to Sister Beth's instructions.

"Heel-toe. Heel-toe. That's it. Heel on the brake. Toe on the gas."

Gail downshifted around the bend, then gunned the straightaway. She took a deep breath.

"That felt great! Where did you learn to drive like that?"

"My daddy was one of those Thunder Road types. He used to do a fair job of importing corn liquor in the back of his old Dodge." Sister Beth adjusted her wimple. "That man lived to the hilt. His only problem was that he ran on the wrong fuel—alcohol, cigarettes, and wild women." She lifted her eyes to the heavens. "I decided to choose a different grade of gasoline oil . . . Hit it, Gail."

Gail leaned back, flattening her toe against the gas pedal.

Thirty miles and three steer-in-the-direction-of-the-slides later, Gail turned to Sister Beth. "What if Bud calls and I'm not there?"

"What if he doesn't call and you're there?"

"You're right."

· · · ·

"Anyway, he looks like the decent type."

"Bud is pretty decent." Gail smiled and turned toward Sister Beth. "This is wonderful. I don't remember the last time I hung out with another girl."

Gail blushed as soon as she realized what she had said. "Sister, I didn't mean . . ."

"Forget it." Sister Beth pointed out the window. "What do you think?"

Both sides of the road were blooming with nursery flowers raised by the nursery cooperative for florist shops across the world. The brilliant colors were woven together like a spectacular quilt. Gail thought it was the most beautiful thing she had ever seen.

Under the watchful eye of the elders and women gathered in the clearing outside the thorn fence, the laibon approached an older woman muttering wildly to herself. She quieted down when he reached her side, then covered her head with a burlap sack. He escorted her to a long, narrow hole recently dug out in the ground. A mound of fresh dirt stood nearby.

At that moment, Bud and Liz walked into the clearing, followed closely by Opana, the glowing child, whom Bud had nicknamed Hope.

"Just a minute, Budweiser."

"Do you mind? We've only got a few minutes. I need to talk to my wife." Bud had waited patiently all morning until he was certain they could leave Kimo for a few minutes while Liz helped him radio Gail at the clinic.

Then Bud stopped in his tracks. The laibon was laying an old woman in a shallow grave next to a mound of dirt.

"What is he doing?!"

"It's been twenty years since I've seen this," Liz whispered, hardly able to contain her excitement.

"It's not your normal Maasai practice," she explained. "This laibon must've added it to his bag of tricks."

"Added what?"

"Burying someone alive to treat dementia."

. . . .

The laibon lowered a goat, very much alive, wriggling desperately inside a large burlap bag, into the hole next to the woman. Then he gestured to the elders, who began slowly refilling the hole with dirt.

"Shouldn't we stop them?" asked Bud. He stepped toward the grave.

"Of course not. He's treating her by the best available means—by isolating the patient, then depriving the brain of adequate oxygen."

"You make it sound like primitive shock therapy."

"It's more than that. Look around. This is the laibon's study, his operating suite, and his cathedral. He treats the mind, body, and spirit in an all-encompassing way."

"If he's such a hotshot, what are we doing here?"

"He's not always right."

"Does she know that?"

"Sounds like you're having a real adventure, Bud." Gail fingered the strand of pearls over her white blouse. She sat at Sister Jill's desk and spoke into the microphone of the shortwave radio.

"We came here to be together," said Bud. "I don't blame you for being disappointed." Bud was a hundred and twenty kilometers due east in a cow pasture. He brushed several flies away from his face as he stared out the copilot's window. He tried to ignore the cows' eyes watching him so intently.

Hope sat in the cockpit, playing with the steering wheel.

"Disappointed, frustrated—yes. Mad? No. I married a doctor, remember?"

"Yeah, I remember."

"How's he doing?"

"He's made progress, but it's too early to say. We'll see how he does tonight." He smiled at Hope, who was singing like a songbird. "Hey, I met the most beautiful little girl this morning."

"Who is she?" A car horn tooted in the background. Gail called out the window, "I'll be right there!"

"Gail, what's going on?"

"Oh, that was Sister Beth. She's waiting for me in the car."

· · · ·

"Isn't it kind of late to be going out?"

"No. The party at the coffee plantation doesn't start for another hour."

"Party?" Bud asked weakly.

. . . .

SIX

Kimo would recover. Just like the oloiboni said he would. However, Bud wasn't so sure about his own prognosis. Bud, Liz, and all of the Maasai gathered to celebrate in a small clearing outside the thorn fence. They watched as three tall, lithe, bare-chested warriors held a prized bull and suffocated it with the ceremonial calfskin.

Bud and Liz sat rigidly on grass mats. Their hair was slicked back with bright red ocher. Cow fat greased their faces like white suntan lotion. An elder walked up to Bud, took a long sip from a gourd, then blew a large mouthful of milk into Bud's face.

"Whoa!" Bud shouted in surprise. "Are they making this up as they go along?"

"It's a special blessing," whispered Liz, tilting her face up to receive her milk spritz. The warm, sour liquid streamed down her glowing face.

"I never thought I'd live to see the day that I'd become an honorary Maasai," she said. "Unless they find out I'm a woman first."

Bud stared down at her bosom. "Oh, God . . ."

A few minutes later, he and Liz knelt down in front of the freshly sliced-open cow's stomach, then closed their eyes and slurped hot and gritty cow's blood. That was when Bud stopped analyzing what was happening to him. He let go. It felt good to relax. There was a lot to be said for devastating fatigue and jet lag on top of three of the early warning signs of sunstroke. As long as they didn't try to bury him alive, he was game.

An elder passed Bud a gourd and motioned for him to drink. Without hesitating, he lifted the gourd to his lips and began guzzling like a freshman during pledge week.

"Whoa!" His head was spinning.

"Pass it to me, Budweiser."

"One more," he said, taking a longer hit. "Gotta build my fluids up. I'm dehydrated."

"You've had enough." She took the calabash of honey beer away.

At the end of the ceremony, the elders presented their new honorary Maasai "brothers" with an ostrich-feather headdress, buffalo-hide shield, long-bladed spear, and a young, willing Maasai woman from their age group.

Cradling all but the last of their presents in their arms, Liz bowed and spoke for both of them in Swahili. "We receive your gifts with much honor. However, it is late, and we must return home."

"What did you say?" Bud asked.

"I very politely turned down the girls. You ready to go?"

"No, I want one."

"Let's go, Budweiser."

"Not yet."

As the elders watched attentively, Bud stepped forward, scanning the faces in the crowd. He saw the beaming face of the old woman who'd been buried with the goat. Dusty, but in fine spirits. Finally Bud saw her—Hope. He pointed the child out to the crowd.

"Tell them I want her," he said to Liz.

Hope's mother angrily shook her head.

"No . . . no . . . wait," said Bud. "Listen. Hope is very sick. More sick than Kimo. I know she doesn't look sick, but she is. Inside. Here." He dropped everything in his arms, and spread his hands over his chest.

"Every day, every hour, she's getting sicker. Soon she won't be able to walk." He stared back at Liz. "Are you getting all this?"

Liz wasn't sure. Budweiser was certainly tenacious for a tourist

. . . .

doctor, but he was wound too tight. In the back of her mind, she feared he might be stripping his screws.

"I can help Hope if you let me take her to America where I live. That's what I'm asking you."

Liz was quiet for a moment.

"Are you sure about this, Budweiser?"

"Ask them."

When Liz translated his request, the elders glanced at each other and murmured a few throaty ticks and tocks, which sounded fairly agreeable to Bud. The child's mother, Pika, added her harmonious voice. Even the laibon seemed to be part of the majority.

Finally a distinguished elder answered Liz. "The elders thank you for your generosity. And they say that they are in complete agreement. The answer is no."

Bud shouldered his disappointment, buzzing head, and armload of Maasai artifacts back to Liz's airplane. He trudged behind Liz and one of the tall, lithe warriors.

The afternoon sun reflected brightly on the wings of the little Cessna. Forty hours earlier they had touched down on this remote little pasture. Little more than forty-eight hours since Bud had contemplated African soil from a seat behind the Beating Around the Bush photo safari group.

He bore little resemblance to the clean, presentable doctor who could have walked off the page of an upscale clothing catalog. But two days ago he wasn't an honorary Maasai brother. Nor was he wearing an ostrich-feather headdress that barely shielded the equatorial sun from his bloodshot eyes and ocher-streaked face. He was still wearing the same wrinkle-free travel clothes. But now they were studded with mud, cattle dung, sour milk, and dried blood.

A few minutes later, when a diesel tour bus was seen chugging across the plains toward them, no one seemed more excited than Bud.

"Slow down!" yelled Gordon Sharpe. He steadied himself at the front of the bus, and raised his binoculars. He could make out the details of the bush plane, the flying doctor, a Maasai warrior, and a

· · · ·

thirty-something white guy leaping up and down with a long spear, buffalo-hide shield, and black bag.

Cruising the bush in a safari bus was like deep-sea fishing, thought Gordon. You never knew what you might drag up next.

"Ho!" Gordon shouted.

"Where?" said Moses, the driver.

"Steady ahead."

Bud couldn't believe his eyes. As the bus lurched to a dusty stop in front of them, and the doors whooshed open, Gordon Sharpe materialized on the carpeted steps like a long-lost friend.

"Gordon!" Bud shouted. "I don't believe it!"

Gordon flashed a brilliant smile. He was well known in these parts. But he couldn't remember every bush drunk he'd met.

"Good to see you, Buddy. How you been?"

"Great! Liz and I just became honorary Maasai." He paused. Where were his manners? "Liz, this is Gordon. Gordon, Liz. That's Sanko. Sanko, Gordon."

"Let's go home, Budweiser," Liz whispered. Now she was really beginning to worry about the doctor's judgment.

Sanko's guard was up, too. The persons in the bus weren't to be trusted. He watched alertly for any sudden movements. He didn't have long to wait.

Ernest Hollings slipped to the front of the bus armed with his Canon SX. While his fellow safari members sat back engorged from the all-you-can-eat smorgasbord at the Canopy Restaurant, Ernest tiptoed in his white socks to the bus's open door. There he had the poor judgment to point his 300mm zoom lens at the Maasai warrior. Ernest got one shot off.

Without hesitating, Sanko launched his spear at Ernest.

In a horrible second it was all over. The spear crashed into the windshield, shattering half the shatterproof glass.

Ernest sat on the bottom step of the bus, shaken but unhurt.

"What did I tell you?" Gordon screamed at the crestfallen Ernest. "What did I tell you? Never, ever, ever take a photo of an ethnic person without authorization from me!"

· · · ·

35

Moses, Peter, and the safari members stared at the spear lodged in the smashed windshield.

Yesterday, a warrior assaulting a tourist bus would have caused Bud some concern. Today Bud had one overriding concern: to return to his wife ASAP. He wasn't even sure he could trust Liz. During the hike back to the Cessna, she had hinted at stopping on the way home for a routine inoculation at another remote village.

"Can I ask you a favor?" Bud asked Gordon.

Gordon smiled uneasily at the white guy's long spear. One more confrontation on this safari and it'd be goodbye Gordon. He was already down one passenger, Number Thirty, and now a windshield.

"Sure, Buddy." Gordon flashed two rows of gleaming teeth. "Anything you want."

"Can you drop me off at the Kilbezi Clinic?"

"Sure, we pass right by it."

Moses shook his head incredulously. They had one more scheduled stop to make that afternoon. The Kilbezi Clinic was forty kilometers out of their way.

The wind whistled in through the shattered windshield of the bus.

"Hey, Buddy." Gordon leaned over the aisle to check on Bud. The man looked like he'd been run over by a speeding cow.

Behind him, tour members pinched their nostrils shut and shrank in their seats.

"Hey, Buddy?" Gordon nudged him gingerly.

It was no use. The bush zonker was cutting silent Z's. Gordon hoped he would sleep through the next stop on the itinerary—a visit to an "authentic" Maasai village.

SEVEN

"No, no, no!" shouted Zach Tyler.

Six Maasai warriors lowered their videocams. What now?

The global village was hard at work. Zach's classroom was a clump of trees on the edge of a wide grassy plain. The Maasai were close enough to the village to respond to any emergency, but far enough away from their girlfriends to pay attention to Zach Tyler.

"No zoom. No in and out, remember!" The warriors were fascinated by the way the image changed in the viewfinder.

Zooming, as Zach knew, was the trademark of the video-idiot.

"No zoom," the Maasai warriors repeated. They smiled, shifting from one leg to the other. They were beginning to understand "zoom," "pan," and "closeup."

Zach walked behind them, checking out each warrior's shot of the wide plain. "You're panning too fast," he cautioned. He gripped one warrior's arm to demonstrate how slowly to pan. "Nice and easy."

The warrior hesitated. There was a shout from the village. The other tall, lithe warriors stood very erect, listening carefully.

It was an emergency.

Zach wasn't surprised. Emergencies ran the gamut from missing cows to marauding lions to lonely girlfriends. Warriors were like firemen, always on call. They raced away with their videocams in one hand, scooping up their spears in the other.

. . . .

"Stop and shoot!" Zach called out behind them. They had a bad habit of trying to record live action while running and leaping.

As the tour bus bumped and swayed over the washed-out road leading to the global village, Gordon stood behind the driver and spoke soothingly into a microphone. "Welcome to a traditional Maasai village . . ."

From the back of the bus, Gordon heard a chorus of rowdy boos.

"We already got a Maasai souvenir in the windshield!"

"Let's get the hell out of Dodge!"

"My son's a lawyer!"

"C'mon, people. This is a certified Beating the Bush stop. We've got sanitary facilities here. Surely you don't believe we'd install clean restrooms here if we thought this was going to be a trouble spot!"

The rowdies grew silent.

"We've taken care of everything. We pay the village a generous royalty for photographs. All you have to think about is your f-stop." Gordon was gratified to see a few pith helmets bobble up and down in a more affirmative spirit. "You'll also find plenty of beautiful native jewelry for sale."

Outside the bus, Maasai women were running to take positions beside blankets filled with beaded jewelry, six-foot lion spears that screwed apart and fit in suitcases, imprinted tea towels, and coasters.

Extras drifted toward their positions in the village. Maasai elders traded comfortable slippers for old leather sandals and pulled old blankets over khakis and T-shirts. The women quickly attached the heavy earrings that stretched their earlobes to fantastic lengths.

The bus doors whooshed open. No one moved.

Gordon grimaced at Bud, who was curled up asleep in a front seat of the bus. "C'mon, folks," he pleaded. "I think we could all use a little fresh air, don't you?"

Bruce Deterding, Lincoln, Nebraska, stood up and slung the wide red, white, and blue strap of his Minolta over his thick, hairy neck. "C'mon. Let's get us some head shots."

Slowly, one by one, the group filed out of the bus.

. . . .

"Fill up on the jewelry, ladies," Gordon called out behind them. "It's absolutely the cheapest anywhere in Maasailand. At these prices, you don't want to forget anybody back home."

This was one of Gordon's favorite stops. His kickback on jewelry sales alone was twenty percent.

Loomo darted out of the video hut and down the trail to intercept Zach Tyler. After the incident over the video business, Loomo thought it best to shield the idealistic Zach from his other commercial enterprises. Like his contract with Gordon Sharpe. The tourists dropped a few hundred in hard currency every time they visited the village.

Loomo held up his hands as Zach marched down the path toward him. "Nothing to worry about, old friend. Tiko's goat kicked over a cooking pot."

"Let's document it," said Zach. The warrior cameramen needed the practice.

"Zach, let's talk."

"About what?"

"Promise you won't have a cow."

"I promise."

"Before we become a truly global village, we need to pay the bills."

"What bills?"

"I mean, our dues." As Loomo described his arrangements with Gordon and the photo safari, Zach's eyes bulged. Finally he could take it no longer. He hurried to the village to see for himself.

"Zach, be cool!" Loomo threw up his hands. "Tourists scare easily."

Bud opened his eyes. He was lying across two seats on an empty bus. Outside, Maasai women were holding up necklaces and beer coasters to a crowd of jostling pith helmets.

Americans were fanning out through the village armed with their cameras. Three Maasai women posed happily, their slim bodies draped with calfskin dresses and adorned with beaded necklaces, bracelets, anklets. Cameras rolled and clicked all around them.

. . . .

The tourists shifted their attention when they heard the sounds of running footsteps.

"Warriors," Gordon called out eagerly. A few of the tourists headed for the bus.

It was certainly dramatic. Africa's most feared and revered warriors, the Maasai, racing down the path toward them with long-bladed spears. Their handsome features and muscular builds, their reddish togas and red-stained pigtails were made for Kodachrome.

At closer range, the eyes of the tourists locked on the warriors' latest weapons: brand-new Sony 8mm videocams.

"What do they think they're doing?"

"They're shooting *us!*"

"Ahhhh!"

The Maasai cameramen slowed to a steady walk and aimed at the tourists. Ladies with big hair came into focus. A wide angle of tourists wearing pith helmets, dark sunglasses, and pressed khakis.

"What the hell?" said Gordon. His flock of tourists lowered their cameras uncertainly as they stared uncomfortably into the lenses of the six warrior cameramen. "Whose photo op is this?"

The warriors moved in a tight formation. One crouched low and went in for a tight shot of a marine-style crewcut. Another went for a medium shot of a woman's earring in the shape of a native American Indian tomahawk.

Three warriors surrounded an American vet with a tattoo of a nude pinup girl on his arm, then moved quickly on to the woman next to him . . . tiny pierced ears, painted lips, and penciled-in eyebrows.

The tourists took a deep breath.

"Return fire!" shouted Deterding, Lincoln, Nebraska, aiming his Minolta.

Click click click.

The American tourists moved into line, photographing the ankle bells around the warriors' dusty ankles, handmade leather sandals with Michelin tire soles, knotty marathon runners' calves decorated with ashes and clay.

"What in God's name . . ." Zach Tyler stood at the edge of the

. . . .

village. The warriors were going head to head with the American tourists. Is this how wars would be fought in the future age of the global village?

"Uncle Zach?" Bud said in disbelief. He stumbled through the crowded clearing toward his former Lufthansa aislemate.

A tourist dropped to his knees for a low-angle shot of a beaded belt worn over a warrior's buttocks.

Another tourist made a flanking motion. Long, plaited hair. Neck-band made from a goat's stomach. Beaded necklaces crisscrossing a chest.

A warrior's closeup revealed an American elder nervously prying open a child-safety cap, and putting two capsules between snow-white dentures.

"Zach Tyler?"

"Dr. Payne?" Zach's face filled with concern. "What happened?"

"In the bush. Medical emergency." Bud's head was spinning. "Catch ride with Gordon. Clinic. Long story."

"You're witnessing a historic moment, Dr. Payne. We're passing through the age of tourism to usher in the age of the global village."

"Oh?"

"You don't look so hot. How about a cold drink?"

"Please."

Bud followed Zach down the trail around the village, then toward a completely hidden Quonset hut.

"C'mon in," said Zach. "Is diet Coke all right? It's all I drink, but I still can't lose any of this." He grabbed his belly. "Go figure."

The hut was a miniature warehouse of sound and video equipment, complete with a full editing board and animation software. The 27-inch monitor along the wall was tuned to GNN Headline News. The Hollywood Minute.

"Loomo, this is Dr. Payne. He's the American doctor I told you about."

Loomo greeted Bud warmly. "The one who helped smuggle the satellite linkup and videocams through customs?"

"That's the one."

. . . .

41

"Nice to meet you, Dr. Payne."

Bud held the cold diet Coke in both hands and took a long sip. "That's not exactly what happened."

Loomo wasn't listening. He watched a film clip starring a well-known American comedian stumble along a sandy beach after a sunbathing beauty. Land mines were exploding all around them. *Beach Blast* was described by the reviewer as "an action-packed comedy following the antics of an American bachelor searching for a Number Ten in postwar Kuwait."

"What's a number ten?" asked Loomo.

Zach was still going on about the global village, oblivious to the Hollywood Minute that was diverting both Loomo and Bud.

Finally, Bud belched loudly and said, "I've gotta go."

"How would you like to see a rough cut of the first Maasai Minute?"

"I've got to catch my bus."

Zach and Loomo followed Bud through the photographers rumbling outside the village.

"In the age of the global village, doctors will be able to treat patients without ever leaving their office," Zach said, huffing and puffing. "You'll be able to diagnose a heart problem, assist in surgery, and do follow-up from a thousand miles away."

"Number Thirty!" Gordon shouted at Zach. His tourists were restless, confused, and abandoning the souvenirs. "It's you! Number Thirty!"

Loomo felt confused. If the American bachelor on the beach was searching for a number ten, what could be inferred from Zach being a number thirty?"

"This used to be an authentic Maasai village!" said Gordon. "Now look at it!"

Fearlessly the warriors walked into the tourists' line of flash for tighter closeups. Masonic rings. Moon watches. Gold fillings. Pearl earrings. Support stockings. Air Jordans. A tattoo of the Cleveland Indians mascot.

"The era of tourism has created an underclass of pawns," Zach

. . . .

said to Bud confidentially. "No wonder Gordon's upset. He's a third-rate colonial master."

Zach shouted at Gordon, "You, safari man, wouldn't know a real village if it walked up and bit you on the rear!" He lowered his voice again to Bud. "Of course, we've had our setbacks."

Without mincing words, he told Bud all about Loomo's video business. Loomo was expecting a huge draw when *Die Hard* played this weekend.

Shaved armpits. Plastic fingernails. Bermuda shorts worn with black stretch socks. White patent leather shoes. Mirrored sunglasses.

When the warriors were less than ten feet away, the tourists broke for the bus, muttering threats intended mostly for Gordon Sharpe.

"Of course, every day is a challenge, Dr. Payne." Zach seemed happy to have someone to confide in.

"Take my plan for telemedicine. I have the equipment in place, but I need professionals on the other end—your end."

"Huh?" Bud wasn't paying attention. Gordon was urging the tour group to reboard the bus. A Maasai cameraman was in his face, but Gordon remained cool. He knew anger didn't play well in closeups.

"Dr. Payne, we need you."

Zach held his arm above the elbow as Bud tried to pull away.

Inside the bus, Gordon whispered sharply to Moses, "Let's get the hell out of this hole."

"What about him?" Moses pointed at Bud.

"Leave him."

Bud heard the bus engine roar to life. "Zach, I need to leave now. I'd like to take my arm with me."

"Dr. Payne, we need this arm to help us achieve our goals."

"Please let go, Zach."

"You'll stay in touch?"

"You have my word."

Moses glanced out his window at Bud, who was running toward the bus as if his life depended on it. Moses' foot was still on the brake as he shifted into low gear, then looked up to see Gordon in the rearview mirror desperately passing out free drink coupons.

. . . .

At the last moment, Moses opened the bus doors and Bud leaped in.

"Thanks for waiting, Gordon." Bud slipped into his seat with a long sigh of relief.

"Next stop," Gordon announced, tossing drink coupons, "an authentic rural clinic."

EIGHT

Late afternoon shadows were falling over the Kilbezi Clinic. Inside the guest cottage, Gail was sitting on the bed writing a letter. She had been disappointed when the flying doctor had returned without her husband. However, Liz had reassured her that he would be arriving at any moment. What were a few more minutes after already being apart from her husband for three days of their four-day vacation?

A loud diesel bus pulled up outside the cottage. It had hardly stopped before it roared off. A moment later the cottage door opened.

Gail stared at the awesome sight filling the doorway. "Bud?" she asked. Then with a giggle, "Bud?"

His ostrich-feather headdress reached to the ceiling as he staggered in with his long spear, buffalo-hide shield, and black medical bag.

She wrinkled her nose. "You smell like fertilizer."

"I can't believe tomorrow is our last day in Kenya," he said, dropping everything on the floor at his feet.

Gail noticed his eyes were dull—the look he got after three sets of tennis in the middle of summer. She stood up carefully, and backed toward the bathroom.

"I can't believe how beautiful you are," he said, stepping toward her.

"Is that blood on your shirt?" Gail reached behind her back, and flipped on the shower. Bud stepped into the walk-in shower, clothes and all.

"What happened out there?"

"They made me an honorary member of the tribe."

The shower had a powerful restorative effect on Bud. Within thirty minutes, he was clean, dressed in fresh clothes, and able to sit down and guide his feet into loafers.

Sitting across from him on the bed, Gail brushed her long, straight hair. He watched each brush stroke, too happy for words to be reunited with the ordinary details of domestic life again.

"Do we have to go to this thing tonight?" he asked.

"It's called a harambee," said Gail. "And we have to go."

"What's a harambee?"

"Officially it means 'Let's all pull together.' Unofficially it means the people have to raise money for all the things the government should provide but can't or won't—like schools, clinics, utilities, and roads."

Gail straightened up. Her hair was full and glossy. She slipped on a new pair of earrings. "How do they look? I bought them during a quick road trip to Nairobi with Sister Beth."

Bud studied the long, dangling earrings. "Part Maasai. Part Modern Museum of Art."

Sister Beth parked the car on the shoulder of the highway. She joined them as they walked toward a few hundred people milling about a bonfire.

"It's just a good old-fashioned hootenanny," said Sister Beth.

Gail linked arms with her while holding hands with Bud. "This is going to be fun!"

Young girls wearing green grass skirts held arms and danced together as the people around them chanted loudly in Swahili. People lined up and moved toward the front where a local politician held out a sisal basket. As the people dropped money into the basket, the well-dressed businessman/politican exhorted the crowd in sing-

. . . .

46

song Swahili to do more, more, and more! He sounded like a speeded-up primitive Baptist, full of the Holy Spirit, smoking out the congregation.

One by one the men, women, and children dropped their coins and bills into the basket as they filed past. Each time they did, they joined the chant, shouting even louder than the orator. A feeble woman shuffled along unnoticed in the dirt. She danced and scratched her private dance in the earth like an old bird. Another well-dressed businessman stepped up and slammed a great wad of bills into the basket. A shock of energy went through the crowd.

"C'mon, Bud." The excitement was getting to Gail. Without hesitating, she led him over to the conga line.

"How much do you have on you?" he asked.

"I didn't bring anything," she said as she twirled around in line. "I thought you did."

Bud flipped open his wallet. Family photos unfolded accordion-style down to his knees. He refolded them, then searched through receipts, notes, library cards, videostore cards, insurance cards, and credit cards. But no shillings or dollars.

In front of him, Gail was moving her body to the beat. She was catching a lot of eyes and smiles. The lady had rhythm. Bud, however, could feel every stiff bone in his body—even on a good night. Everyone was moving. Moving toward the basket, toward the fire, toward the table where three men sorted out change and bills from a pile of money dumped out of the basket.

As Bud and Gail zeroed in on the sisal basket, a commotion arose on the other side of the bonfire. They craned their necks but couldn't see anything. A hush gradually fell over the crowd. Then everyone stepped aside, making room for the tall Maasai warrior. Slowly, one by one, the other Maasai approached the fire. Elders, women, maidens, and children. Kimo walked slowly, supported by two warriors. Finally, the laibon. In his arms he carried the limp body of Hope. Liz wasted no time reaching the laibon's side to check the child's vital signs.

"We need oxygen!"

After a minute, she announced that Hope's vital signs were stable,

· · · ·

but she needed immediate rest and fluids after the long, sixty-kilometer trek to the clinic.

Sister Beth ran toward the Plymouth, where emergency medical supplies were stored in the trunk.

Liz held out her arms, speaking to the laibon in Swahili.

"Please," she said. "She needs our help. Now."

The elders whispered to the laibon. But the healer seemed too deep inside himself to hear. Finally, Kimo gave his permission.

With great reluctance, the laibon lowered Hope into Liz's arms.

"Bud, what's going on?" asked Gail. Then she saw him standing beside the sisal basket.

"Let this be our contribution to the harambee," Bud said loudly, raising his AmEx gold card high in the air. The crowd oohed and aahed as they watched the gold plastic sparkle in the light of the bonfire.

Liz translated for him.

"I appeal one last time to my honorary Maasai family. Let us fly Hope to my country, the U.S.A., for emergency heart surgery. Kimo, she can't live without our medicine. What do you say?"

When Liz finished speaking, the elders glanced at each other. Obviously they had already decided on a course of action.

As the elder spokesman opened his mouth to reply, the laibon interrupted. Pointing his o-rinka baton in Bud's direction, he began shouting angrily at Kimo and the elders.

Finally, Kimo held up his hand. His voice was exceedingly smooth, yet forceful. He seemed tired, but his tremendous strength was stamped on every word and expression. Bud fondly recalled the dreamlike experience in which Kimo spoke English like Cary Grant.

Liz waited until he was finished, then translated.

"He says when he was a warrior, he lived for himself. But he's now at the age when he must become a junior elder, and live for his family. He speaks for his family when he says they trust their honorary brother, and will let him take the child to America for healing. But not alone."

The crowd broke out in loud, sustained applause and cheers.

. . . .

Bud was holding up his hands. "Of course not alone! We want her to be with her mother, or guardian, or whoever you choose."

After Liz translated, Kimo nodded in stern agreement.

The well-dressed businessman stepped out of line and walked toward Bud. He was still mopping his brow from his last contribution.

"Let me be of some assistance," the Kenyan said. "I run a small travel agency in Nairobi. I'd be more than happy to take care of the flight arrangements, Doctor."

In the meantime, Bud introduced Gail to the Maasai. Her earrings were perfect. She greeted Kimo and each Maasai elder. She bent down and hugged Hope, then shook hands with her mother, Pika, and the other women.

Liz took Bud aside. "The child is stable, but we'll watch her in the clinic until she's ready to fly."

"Thanks, Liz."

"I hope you don't think I'm terribly impressed by all this."

"Of course not."

Afterward, the Nairobi travel agent led Bud over to his Mercedes, where he produced a dusty credit card machine from the trunk.

"So, Dr. Payne. What'll it be? First class? Coach? I guarantee the lowest fares in Nairobi. No commission on this."

"How soon can we get her a flight?" Bud asked, handing over the gold card.

The travel agent's smile lit up. "Ah, yes, the gold card." He touched the plastic reverently. "Beautiful." He slipped the card into his credit card machine. "How about we book them for next week? I'll take care of the paperwork at the office. This little girl will be the first Maasai with frequent flyer points, eh?"

Toward the end of the evening, Bud took Gail's hand and they slipped inside a one-room schoolhouse across from the huts. The schoolhouse was dark and sparsely furnished. Bud kissed Gail without hurry. The sounds of the harambee in full swing reached them across the field. When he kissed her neck, he heard the tinkle of the Maasai earrings.

Gail had never thought of Bud as the heroic or adventurous type.

. . . .

He had never set out to achieve fame or fortune. Yet now he would be returning home as an honorary Maasai warrior. Bud spread his jacket out on the floor. Gail lay down and smiled as she felt his weight slowly press against her. They closed their eyes for just a moment. On their first—and last—night alone, neither wanted to be the first to break the spell.

NINE

Bud slowly opened his eyes. It was still dark. Something was crawling over his chest. Something familiar. The little nocturnal creature nestled between him and Gail, no doubt seeking warmth from their bodies. He drifted back to sleep with a peaceful feeling.

Gail awoke a few minutes later to high-pitched chirping sounds. When she tried to snuggle closer to Bud, she found the small warm body between them.

"Good morning, Mommy," said Lisa, seven, lying between them in the king-size bed. She was dressed in cowboy hat, pink tutu, and roller skates.

"Good morning, sweetheart," whispered Gail, closing her eyes. "Give me a kiss. Now let's see who can sleep the longest."

"Mommy, the alarm's ringing."

"That's okay, Lisa. That's what alarms do. They ring."

After midnight last night, Gail and Bud had taken a cab home from Atlanta's international airport. An hour later they dumped all the bags and suitcases in the den, checked in on their sleeping children, then climbed into bed knowing that they would return to work in a few hours feeling complete exhaustion from their vacation.

Bud rolled over and turned off the alarm. He forced his eyes open and saw his son standing next to the bed.

. . . .

Douglas, eleven, wore the large Giants starter jacket that he had received for Christmas. He held up the small, exquisite carving of an eland that Gail had picked out for him from a Nairobi sidewalk vendor.

"Is this for me or Lisa?" Douglas asked without a trace of enthusiasm.

"That's yours."

"Thanks." Douglas palmed the eland. "Maybe next year you can go to Japan and bring back a new Nintendo game."

"Bud, it's the office!" Gail poured two cups of coffee as she pressed the receiver of the cordless phone against her robe.

Bud moved quickly into the kitchen, clipping his beeper onto his belt. He reached for the phone, then his coffee cup. "Yeah, we got back late last night," he said, smiling at Gail.

Gail leaned against the countertop and watched the children. Seated at the table, they were eating fluorescent green breakfast cereal. Her mother must have let the children pick out the groceries while they were gone.

"I'll see you in twenty minutes." Bud rolled his eyes at Gail, then added, "Okay, fifteen."

"Do you have time for breakfast?" she asked. It was only a eight-minute drive to the hospital—six minutes if you caught all the green lights.

"Sure . . . Ernie says last week was a nightmare. The pollen counts were way over last year's highs."

"Good morning, good morning," chimed Lilly as she walked up into the kitchen. In her mid-sixties, Gail's mother used more makeup and hair spray now than she ever did the whole time she was married to Gail's father. The divorce had become final last year.

"Mom, thanks so much for taking care of the kids."

Lilly stood behind the children and smoothed down Lisa's hair. "Your kids are . . ."

Douglas and Lisa held their breath as their grandmother searched for the right words.

". . . the sweetest, most responsible children I've ever seen."

· · · ·

"Whew," sighed Douglas. "Thanks, Grandlilly."

"Lilly, we'll hold a full debriefing later," said Bud.

"My pleasure. Now, I wrote down all your messages and put the mail in the den."

"How are the tulips?" asked Gail.

"Perfectly ready to burst into a cavalcade of glorious color." Lilly smiled ironically. "I believe that's what I told the magazine editor who called to say they definitely want to come by and take some pictures next week."

"The *Backyard Magazine?*" asked Gail excitedly.

"Something silly like that." She swung her purse over her arm and waved goodbye. "Gotta run. Call me and tell me all about it when the dust settles."

Gail sipped coffee as she gazed out the window at the backyard, her crowning achievement.

Flower beds filled with thousands of tulips, daffodils, lilies, and irises were spread out over a gently sloping grass lawn dotted with ornamental shade trees and hedges. Highlighting the garden was an exquisite Italian fountain surrounded by an award-winning rose garden.

Gail pressed the switch marked Fountain next to the one marked Garbage Disposal. The fountain sent up a plume of sparkling water into a bowl of pink marble, then flowed into a miniature pond of waterlilies.

Bud answered the phone on the third ring. "Hello, Joyce . . . Oh, I'm sorry to hear that." He cupped the phone and said to Gail, "Strep throat. Again. Can you car pool this morning?"

Five minutes later, the automatic garage door whooshed open on the Payne' three-car garage. Bud and Gail backed their Saab and Volvo, respectively, down the driveway. At the street, everyone waved good-bye, then went their separate ways.

. . . .

TEN

Deborah Miller Teagarden, the receptionist for Bud's group practice, was reaching for the phone as Bud entered the office. "Welcome back, Dr. Payne."

"Thanks. How's everybody doing?"

"Do you really want to know?"

"Do I have time?"

"No."

"I didn't think so."

Waving a thick stack of index cards in the air, Dr. Ernest Houck stepped out of his office. "Hey, Bud. You ready? I've got a tonsillectomy in five minutes."

"I thought we stopped removing tonsils years ago."

"Yeah, but the kids look so cute without them. C'mon . . ."

Out of the corner of his eye, Bud saw a tall doctor walk past them in the corridor.

"Was that Dr. Chandler?" Bud asked Deborah.

"Unfortunately." Chandler, the cardiac surgeon, might win an award for best dressed but would never receive a vote for congeniality. He was notorious for his frostbitten manners to patients and colleagues alike.

"Ernie, I'll be right back," Bud called out as he hurried out the door.

. . . .

A few seconds later he was matching Dr. Chandler stride for stride down the pale green, fluorescent-lit corridor.

"Jerome, what a coincidence. I was going to call you later."

"Lucky me," said Chandler. "What's the occasion?"

"Have you ever heard of the Maasai tribe?"

"No," Chandler replied. "I'm a little behind on my *National Geographics.*"

Bud plowed ahead, undaunted by Chandler's deadly sarcasm. "The reason I'm bringing this up is because I've got a new patient. A little Maasai girl with mitral valve regurge. Would you consider donating surgical services?

"Rheumatic heart disease?" Chandler glanced at Bud in disbelief. "You're bringing a tribal girl over here for heart surgery?"

"That's right. Next week."

Chandler started chuckling to himself.

Bud asked, "What's so funny?"

"Why is it every time a doctor goes to Africa he starts acting like Albert Schweitzer?"

"I don't know, Jerome," Bud said. "Maybe it's the same reason why every time you ask a cardiac surgeon to do a pro bono case for an indigent patient he gets defensive and changes the subject."

Chandler clenched his jaw shut and kept on walking.

"Jerome, I asked you because you're the best," Bud explained. "And I thought you must be getting bored with doing bypasses all the time. Rheumatic heart disease might be a nice change of pace."

Chandler stopped in the hallway. He sighed as he rested his hand against the door marked MEN.

"I'll tell you what, Bernard. If you can get the bean counter in administration to underwrite the child's hospitalization, I'll do it." Then he shook his head. "But I'll bet the house he says 'no.' "

After dropping the kids off at school, Gail changed into her overalls, straw hat, and gardening gloves. She walked down the granite steppingstones into the backyard garden with much anticipation. And relief. Some flowers had already blossomed, and the rest were bursting at their green seams, giving a hint of the glories to come.

· · · ·

She walked among the flower beds, happily inspecting the landscape that she had worked so hard to create. One day, perhaps, she might turn her passion for landscaping into a business. With a master's degree in fine arts, and years of gardening experience, she felt eminently qualified. The profile in *Backyard Magazine* wouldn't hurt, either.

Gail sat down on a black wrought-iron bench beneath the towering oak to contemplate the garden around her. Moments later, she heard grunting from overhead. The neighbor's Vietnamese potbellied pig was dangling in a climbing harness from the oak tree.

"Peewee?" She followed the pig's harness and rope with her eyes and saw that they were attached buddy-system-style to her neighbor Fanny Butler, dressed in full tree-climbing gear. Fanny, in her late fifties, lowered herself from the immense white oak with ropes and pulleys. Fanny's predilection for alternative new-age lifestyles was the most consistent thing about her. As usual, she was dressed in the latest fashions for teenage girls—in this case, tank top and purple bicycling pants. Unlike most fiftyish women wearing sixteen-ish girls' clothes, Fanny looked good. Her green eyes sparkled with intelligence.

"Gail, I didn't know you were getting back so soon." Fanny kicked away from the tree and dangled in midair. "I hope you don't mind."

"Of course I don't mind, Fanny. I'm glad someone is using these trees besides the birds and squirrels."

"We haven't touched ground for two days and nights." Peewee grunted in confirmation. "Gail, until you've slept in the crotch of a white oak a few hundred feet off the ground, you don't know what real security is."

"How's Bertram?"

"Bertram is packing for some golf tournament in Scotland." Fanny pushed off the tree and swung lower until she reached the ground." After all those years of his practicing law, I thought I'd finally see my husband during retirement. I was wrong. I'm spending my golden years in a tree with a potbellied pig."

Bertram Marshall Butler was a retired corporate lawyer who

wielded considerable power on six boards of directors, including the board of trustees at Bud's hospital. He spent most of his free time at the Indian Mounds, a local golf resort designed to enhance the ancient Indian burial mounds scattered about its fairways.

"So, how was the African honeymoon?" Fanny pushed back her long auburn hair from her face.

"It was fun"—Gail hesitated, deciding how much to tell—"but we more or less went our separate ways."

"Sounds familiar."

"Bud became an honorary Maasai warrior."

"Maasai?" Fanny asked alertly.

"You've heard of them?"

"Of course. An 'intelligent people who have deliberately chosen to retain their own way of life.' Evelyn Waugh. 1960."

"Did Waugh happen to mention anything about burying people alive?"

Bud's description of the laibon burying the old woman alive made a vivid impression on Gail.

"No." Fanny's eyes lit up. "Tell me more."

Bud stood next to the open door of Richard Moorehead's administrative office. Richard was talking into his intercom, but seemed preoccupied with a tray of hospital food. In particular, a bowl of green Jell-O cubes.

"And Chris. . . . Let's run a cost analysis on eliminating the lettuce under the Jell-O. . . ."

When Richard saw Bud, he waved him toward a chair in front of his boat-size mahogany desk.

"Sit down, Dr. Payne. My door is always open for you doctors. Like I say, you run the hospital, not me. Now, what can I help you with?"

The intercom buzzed. Richard leaned forward and answered it.

"Dean Bagwell says the limo is waiting out front."

"Tell Dean Bagwell I'll be a little late for the memorial service for Dr. Stevens." He grinned at Bud. "Dr. Stevens won't mind."

"I know you're busy so I'll get right to the point," said Bud. "I've

. . . .

already met with Dr. Chandler, cardiac surgery. We've got a little Maasai girl from Kenya who needs emergency heart surgery. She arrives next week."

"That's great, Dr. Payne," said Richard. "Hospitals are climbing all over each other to get a piece of the international health-care pie."

Bud leaned forward in the creaking leather chair. "You don't understand. The child belongs to a tribe of seminomadic herdsmen. Would Tully Hospital be willing to underwrite her stay?"

Richard smiled and held up both hands like a used car salesman resisting his customer's low offer. "I can't do it."

"Why not?"

"You know what the bottom line is—occupancy rate. Ours is down twenty percent since St. Mary's started their Tammy Tonsils and Ernie Earache ad campaign. We're being hammered—absolutely nailed to the wall—by Tammy and Ernie."

"This is life or death," Bud replied evenly. "I'm already flying the child over from Kenya. I can't afford to pay for her hospitalization, too."

"I wish I could help, but . . ." Richard tapped his pencil against his teeth. A strange gleam came into his eyes. "Wait a minute . . . life or death . . . A little shepherd girl from the plains of Kenya . . ."

He leaned excitedly over his desk and punched the intercom as he whispered to Bud, "The timing might be just right."

"You'll sponsor her?" asked Bud.

Richard spoke into the intercom, "Linda, get me marketing-public relations." Afterward he ran his fingers through his red pompadour and gazed fondly at Bud.

"You might be right, Dr. Payne. Hosting this child could turn out to be a lovely humanitarian gesture."

Deborah held up the phone up as Bud rushed out of his examining room.

"Kenya, on line one," said Deborah.

"Hello?" Bud said. "Hello?"

. . . .

"Budweiser! Greetings from Kilbezi," Liz shouted from the clinic's radio room. In the background Bud could hear the sisters buzzing with excitement at the news.

"How is she, Liz?"

"She's fine. Don't worry. She'll be arriving next Monday. On Flight 611. But get this . . ." A burst of static was followed by a heavy click. They were disconnected.

Bud caught Deborah's eye. "We lost the connection. But I got the day and the flight number."

Inside the radio room, the sisters expressed their disappointment as Liz hung up the phone.

"Let's ring him again," said Liz.

Suddenly, the shortwave radio came alive: "Kilbezi Clinic. Kilbezi Clinic. Emergency dispatch."

Sister Jill swiveled her chair over to the mike. "Kilbezi Clinic. Go ahead."

"Stand by for emergency medical request."

Minutes later Liz rushed toward the battered Cessna with Sister Beth hot on her heels. "Don't worry. I'll call him as soon as I get back. But let's hope his heart is in better shape than the child's."

Later that evening, as Bud and Gail were getting the children ready for bed, Lisa asked her father for a good night story.

Bud told them about a little girl who lived near Mount Kilimanjaro. "Every day she helped her mother with her chores. She milked the goats, fetched fresh water home, and helped her mother cook."

Lisa was thrilled.

Douglas was also listening. "Do lions ever attack the village and carry off the little girls in their mouths?"

"No, the village is guarded by tall warriors who are expert lion killers with their long-bladed spears."

"Go on, Dad."

"Well, one day a doctor visited her village and he listened to her heart."

"That's you. You're the doctor!" shrieked Lisa.

. . . .

59

"When he found out how sick she was, the doctor asked the little girl's family if she could come to America for open-heart surgery. And guess what they said?"

"Buzz off," said Douglas.

"Guess what they said the second time he asked?"

"Yes!" cried Lisa.

"That's right. And when the doctor came back to America, he asked a busy heart surgeon if he would help. And guess what he said?"

"How much?" said Douglas.

"He said yes!" Lisa called out.

"That's right. Then the doctor asked the big bad hospital administrator who huffed and puffed and finally—"

"Said yes!" Lisa screamed. "When is she coming, Daddy?"

"When, Bud?" asked Gail, sharing the children's excitement.

"Better get the guest room ready," he said to Gail. "She'll be here next Monday."

ELEVEN

"Action!" shouted Loomo.

Lepa ran frantically through the global village. Glancing back over her shoulder, she nearly died of fright. Her heavy ear ornaments made her lobes twist and bounce as she raced past the huts. Then she stumbled exactly at the spot Loomo had blocked out in rehearsal.

Camera two was ready with a tight shot of her lovely face. Her lips trembled with fear. Her mouth opened wide, revealing missing teeth. She scrambled away, kicking up dirt with her calloused bare feet.

Loomo shouted, "Cut!" The six cameramen, grips, makeup and costume, and extras—all Maasai—simultaneously broke into applause for Lepa. She blushed. The crew was so supportive!

"Take five," Loomo said to his crew. He walked over to Zach, who had wandered into the scene just as Lepa hit her mark in the dirt.

"Yo, Zach."

Zach eyed Loomo's film crew and shook his shaggy head. "This is terrible. Just terrible."

Loomo put his arm around him. Very brotherly he asked, "Zach, *now* what's eating you?"

"I wanted to raise you up. Enlighten you. Not drag you through the wasteland of this . . ." He waved his arms.

Everyone on the set was watching them. They weren't surprised. Loomo had explained to them that Zach was executive producer and it was his job to worry.

"Life is hard," said Loomo. "What's wrong with bringing a little happiness and joy to millions?"

"You're making a slasher film, Loomo," Zach reminded him.

"We're just starting. Give us a chance to grow. You know how distributors are . . ." Loomo's dogeared issue of *Variety* proclaimed that film distributors could never get enough slashers.

"I had a dream, Loomo, that one day we would link up your people with people from all over the world. Here in the birthplace of man, man would be reborn, reunited."

"But, Zach, first we need to pass through our schlock stage."

"That one day we'd reestablish human communication on visual, aural terms. Video and audio . . ."

"I'm with you, Zach, all the way." Loomo brushed a fly off his cheek. "But your people have been making films for eighty years. We've been at it . . . What? Two weeks. Next week, who knows what we'll be doing? Maybe docudramas."

"We have the satellite linkup and GNN." Zach stared at the cloudy sky. "But what do you use it for?"

"Arsenio Hall." Loomo shrugged apologetically. "I'm sorry, Zach. The GNN Hollywood Minute just wasn't enough."

"You can't expect to find global reality on Arsenio."

Loomo eyed the diminishing light in the western sky. "You're right. And I'd really love to talk about global reality, Zach. But right now we only have enough light left for one more exterior shot."

He had in mind a moving, hand-held shot of Lepa's attacker, a crazed American tourist wielding a butcher's knife. The American was played by a junior elder, Doree, covered with a fine white chalk found only on the western slopes of Mount Kilimanjaro, and outfitted in khakis, bush jacket, and sunglasses, topped off with a Beating the Bush pith helmet. The story called for Doree to pursue Lepa over the thorn fence into the Maasai kraal. Lepa would dash into a dung hut. With an eye to Hollywood distribution, Lepa would strip

. . . .

off her clothes as soon as she was safely inside. Then she'd pour cow urine from the calabash all over her glistening body. But suddenly she'd hear a noise above her. Mouse? No, a knife slashing at her through the dung-plastered roof!

On Monday afternoon, under clear skies, the Payne family gathered along the runway at the international airport. Within the hour, the 747 would be discharging its special passengers.

Behind them surged a crowd that was growing larger by the minute. Schoolchildren filed out of yellow school buses. Members from the First Baptist, First Methodist, and First Presbyterian arrived, walking behind banners proclaiming their affiliation like modern-day crusaders. Twelve preschool children carried a banner that was more to the point: "We Love Hope! Suzie's Day Care—We Love to Care For Your Children—1200 First Ave."

Mike's Motors, better known for their men's softball team than for selling reliable autos, offered free hot dogs, popcorn, and balloons to the children. To everyone's delight, The Florida A&M University Rattlers performed a slam-dam version of the Coca-Cola anthem about wanting to buy the world a sweet, caffeine-laced drink.

Without informing Bud, Richard had turned the arrival of the Maasai child into a media circus. Video crews, photographers, journalists fanned through the crowd toward Richard's press conference, located front and center.

"This is truly the age of the global village," Richard said, basking in front of the reporters, shouting to be heard over the marching

· · · ·

band. "And Tully Hospital, a quality health care institution, wants to do its part in helping the less fortunate around the world."

Richard pointed to a raised hand. "Yes?"

"Whose idea was it to bring over the little girl?" asked the reporter.

"It's unfair to single out any one individual. Rather I'd like to salute the Tully board of directors, who had the courage, wisdom, and foresight to embark on this ambitious course of action." Richard gestured toward a group of well-dressed men and women holding plastic drink cups with napkins in their hands.

Gail squeezed Bud's hand. "I didn't hear your name mentioned."

"Thank goodness for that," said Bud.

Soon after the last speech was made by a representative of the World Health Organization, the long-awaited jet taxied down the runway toward them. The FAMU Rattlers thumped into the intro of "Theme from *2001*." Cameramen jockeyed for position behind airport security guards at the head of the crowd. As the music from *2001* rose louder, the airport crew wheeled the universal steps into place. The crowd, estimated at fifteen hundred strong, focused their eyes on the jet door. A flight attendant poked her astonished head out, then ducked back inside.

After a long pause, Pika, Hope's mother, stepped out of the doorway. She carried a large bundle made up of blankets and cooking utensils in her arms. Brass ornaments dangled low from her stretched earlobes. Hope followed a few steps behind her mother. Her eyes filled with wonder at the incredible scene on the runway below her. Everyone was clapping. Bright music filled the shimmering air.

The camera crews swarmed toward the bottom of the steps for a better angle of the radiant little Maasai princess, resplendent in her beaded tiara, necklaces, and calfskin dress. Hope walked slowly, delicately barefooted, down the steps.

"You didn't tell me the kid was so darn photogenic," said Richard, appearing at Bud's side.

The remarkable poise of the mother and child was so captivating, in fact, that they were halfway down the metal steps before anyone

· · · ·

65

in the crowd spotted the old laibon, ducking his head to get through the door of the jet.

Wrapped in his dusty blanket, gripping his rhino-horn baton, the Maasai medicine man fiercely ignored the hubbub generated by his unexpected presence.

"What's he doing here?" Gail whispered to Bud.

"Well, he is the child's personal healer." Bud shrugged. There was nothing they could do about it now.

"I hope he doesn't mind sleeping on a cot in the den. I've got the guest bedroom fixed up for Hope's mother."

"Who is that?" Richard asked Bud.

"The laibon. He's a Maasai healer."

"A witch doctor? Oh, goody." Richard rubbed his hands together. "The Movie of the Week thickens. Bring him to the hospital. We'll show him our magnetic resonance imager." Richard stepped away, followed closely by a staff photographer. "I want a closeup with the girl."

As Pika and Hope neared the bottom of the steps, Bud signaled the hospital ambulance. He couldn't relax until Hope was out of the crowd and resting comfortably at the hospital.

He squeezed Gail's hand. "I'll see you at home after she's admitted and resting comfortably at the hospital."

"Good luck."

"Tell her I said hi!" said Lisa.

Douglas said nothing. He was staring at the top of the stairs, too stunned to do anything but raise his arm and point.

One of the Maasai warriors—his tall, lithe body partially covered by his red togalike wrap, called a shuka, leaned out of the jet's doorway. His hair was pulled back in long braids dyed red with ocher. His legs were decorated with long, squiggly lines made from white ash. He wasn't alone. Behind him two more warriors emerged, leaning against him like affectionate brothers, smiling, enjoying the attention from the crowd.

The crowd continued to stare at the doorway of the jet as, one by one, the rest of the tribe emerged from the airliner. Three women balancing heavy bundles on their heads, and nursing children in

. . . .

their arms. Seven elders. The goat lady. Twelve children ranging from infants to young maidens. Three junior elders in their early thirties. Kimo, wearing a white gauze dressing under his red shuka.

Photographers and cameramen rushed by Richard as the bigger, more sensational, picture unfolded.

"Dr. Payne, who are these people?" Richard hissed, his freckles blending together until his face was the same color as his red pompadour.

"The tribe."

"You flew the entire tribe over here?"

Bud finished counting heads. The Maasai tribe filled the staircase and were forming a sizable group at the bottom of the stairs. "I think so." He shivered ever so slightly as he recalled handing his gold card to the Nairobi travel agent during the harambee.

"I agreed to host the child," said Richard. "But not the entire tribe."

"Mr. Moorehead?" A reporter raised his hand. "I don't see anything about this in the press kit."

"Dr. Payne invited the tribe at his own expense and will be glad to answer any of your questions concerning them. Dr. Payne?" Richard slipped through the reporters as his professional instincts took over. He headed for cover.

"Did you expect these people, Dr. Payne?" asked another reporter.

Bud looked chagrined.

The reporters were getting hungrier by the moment. The airport story had that heady Pulitzer aroma: critically ill African child, endangered ethnic group, profit-hungry private hospital, and yuppie surgeon motivated by what? fame, fortune, and/or the religious right?

"Are they seeking political asylum?"

"Who's sponsoring their visit?"

"Where are they staying?"

"C'mon, Dr. Payne. We've got deadlines just like you. Where's the tribe staying?"

Bud eyed his honorary tribe members, the transport nurse holding open the rear door of the ambulance, and the rise and fall of Hope's chest. "They can stay at my house until—"

"What's the address?"

As the reporters started shouting all at once, Bud held up his hands. "That's the last question. We're going to the hospital now."

Thirty feet away, a flight attendant approached Gail with an armful of spears and buffalo-hide shields.

"I'm sorry. Federal regulations don't permit warriors to carry spears and shields on international flights."

"I think someone has made a big mistake," Gail said softly.

"I'm sorry," said the flight attendant. "I don't make the rules."

THIRTEEN

The ambulance was speeding along I-85 as the transport nurse handed the cellular phone to Bud. Hope's mother and the laibon sat beside Hope. She lay rigidly on the portable bed with a thermometer in her mouth.

"We've got Dr. Chandler," said the nurse.

"Thanks. Let's get blood gases ready, then put in an IV line." Bud took the phone. "Jerome? We're on our way to the hospital with the child. Can you meet us there?"

"No, that's impossible. I'll stop by in the morning," Chandler said into the car's speaker phone. He gripped the wheel of his turbo Porsche the way they had taught him last year at a race driving school in Phoenix, Arizona. Gloria, a professional model friend, sank low in the leather seat beside him, her long legs crossed at the ankles.

"It would put our minds at ease if you could see her for just a minute."

"Impossible. I'm emceeing the AMA's charity fashion show, which starts in exactly twenty minutes." He smiled at Gloria, then checked his teeth in the rearview mirror. His tux alone cost more than the blue-book value of most of the cars he passed on the highway.

"She's been through a lot in the last twenty-four hours," said Bud.

"Oh, Jerome," said Gloria. "I hope she's okay—the poor little thing."

Chandler adjusted his bow tie. "Where exactly are you, Dr. Payne?"

Bud leaned over to see the highway better. "We're on I-85. Just past Exit 61."

"Pull over into the emergency lane. Wait for me."

Swabbing off the inside of Hope's left wrist, the transport nurse took careful aim with the needle. She plunged it deep, trying to locate the radial artery. Finally bright red blood gushed forth into the syringe. The nurse turned around in the moving vehicle and set the vial of blood into a minirefrigerator.

The laibon's eyes bore into her. He gripped his baton tighter. As a child, he had heard stories about a race of people who drank human blood. If these people drank Opana's blood, it would be the same as drinking his blood because they were family. Then they would have power over him. He considered fighting to regain the blood. But there were no warriors to aid him. Instead he would watch, and bide his time.

A beer truck, followed by a convoy of middle-aged bikers, drove past the Porsche parked behind the ambulance in the emergency lane.

Inside, Dr. Chandler leaned over Hope and, tilting her face this way and that, peered closely into her eyes, nose, mouth, and ears. He didn't say anything until he reached behind her left ear.

"Now how did that get there?" He opened his hand and showed Hope the quarter he had magically found behind her ear. Except for a little sleight of hand to loosen up his younger patients, he rarely wasted any time on bedside manner.

Hope glanced nervously at her mother, who stared at the shiny coin that had, until moments ago, gone undetected in her daughter's ear.

The laibon studied the heart healer's extravagant black robes and tails. At first he thought they indicated a very important healer. But now he wasn't so sure—a few moments earlier he had watched the

. . . .

strange specialist try to palm the coin. Surely they hadn't traveled across the ocean for a simple child's trick.

"Let's see if there's any more inside here." Dr. Chandler borrowed Bud's stethoscope, invented several hundred years ago by a fastidious European doctor who disliked touching his ear to sweaty chests.

Dr. Chandler closed his eyes, then delicately moved the steth over the child's bare chest, touching the silver bell here and there . . . point here, counterpoint there . . . listening to the deep echo, the great swooshing symphony of blood through the heart.

He handed the stethoscope back to Bud. "Schedule a heart cath for seven A.M.," he said as he left. "I'll see you then."

The laibon stared at the departing tails of the heart healer. Did he expel the demons from the child with the silver bell worn around his neck? The laibon doubted it. The healer was in too much of a hurry to leave. If he had healed the child, he would have stayed longer to demand his payment.

. . . .

FOURTEEN

"Dr. Payne, you just can't believe how excited we are over our new patient," said Nurse Combs as she pressed the last EKG lead onto Hope's chest. Satisfied, she turned around and watched an orange line spring into action on the monitor.

"Everybody's talking about her. I can't wait to get home and see her on the six o'clock news tonight."

Nurse Combs was missing an excellent opportunity to see Hope right now, Bud thought. Like many other nurses and doctors, she was too busy manning the equipment to pay much attention to the patient.

Bud sat on the bed beside Hope and her mother, who was tenderly stroking her daughter's hand. After getting over the initial shock of a hospital bath, and trading in their calfskin dresses for hospital robes, the Maasai mother and child had begun to relax.

Not the laibon. He stood at the foot of the bed scrutinizing anyone who came close to the child.

The laibon stared without emotion at Opana. He dared not even reach out and touch her ankle. She was plugged in, just like the other instruments in the room. She was hooked to the living organism of the hospital whose walls hummed and throbbed around him.

The child didn't dare move beneath the crisp white hospital sheet. IV tubes were taped to her wrist, and the EKG was wired to her ankles, wrists, and chest. A pulse oximeter was attached to her forefinger, making her finger glow, as well as monitoring her pulse rate and the oxygen in her blood. She was surrounded by wires and monitors that hummed and buzzed like a swamp at night.

The laibon would give the white's cure a chance. Some of their medical customs made sense. The wires were like the cowrie shells that could locate the demons inside her body. The tubes dripped a powerful potion into her arms so that she could fight off more demons.

The only thing he didn't understand was the box mounted over the bed with wires leading to Opana. On the box, he watched a wild dog standing on two legs blow himself to smithereens with explosives as a bird ran by saying *"beep beep."*

Other animals empowered the room as well. Mounted on the wall behind Opana's bed was an immense cutout of a mouse wearing white gloves. Perched on chairs, chest of drawers, and windowsills was an ominous gathering of lions, tigers, bears, giraffes, rhinos, pigs, cats, dogs, and snakes.

In the days before Hope's arrival, mothers from across the metropolitan area had been dropping off plastic bags full of the glassy-eyed stuffed animals. However, because of the fear of spreading infection, the hospital had turned down these used gifts. Instead, surrounding Hope were brand-new stuffed animals donated by local merchants.

Nurse Combs cradled a red-eyed lion cub in her arms as she walked toward Hope. "Ain't he the sweeeetest . . ."

Hope shrank back. She stared helplessly at the lion cub next to Nurse Combs' bosom. In the bush, these wild beasts haunted every waking and dreaming moment.

The laibon watched Nurse Combs with professional interest. She was waving the lion cub in Hope's face. Would the demon show himself? To him, using animals in certain healing procedures was simply a matter of taste. Personally, he preferred using live goats.

"Don't be shy," said the nurse. "It won't bite."

Bud was about to intervene when he heard a woman's voice behind him say, "Excuse me. Can I see that?"

. . . .

Candystriper Cynthia Goodman filled out her pink and white uniform like few young women Bud had ever seen. Usually these volunteer girls were extremely pale, thin, and retiring. In contrast, Cynthia was dark-skinned, statuesque, and confident. Bud liked the way her eyes and mouth worked in full, all-out harmony.

"Thanks much," Cynthia said, accepting the stuffed animal from the nurse, then throwing it into the closet. "This child is from the bush. These are her worst nightmares." As she scooped up the other animals, she turned to Hope and said in fluent Swahili, "Cynthia's here. Don't you worry about a thing, child."

"You speak Swahili?" asked Bud.

"My father is from Kenya," she replied. "When I found out you had a Maasai child here, I came as soon as I could."

She noticed the o-rinka horn that the laibon carried, and carefully chose a few words to address the Maasai healer.

"Do you know who he is?" Bud asked.

"He's a laibon." Cynthia stared at the Maasai with a teasing grin.

"What did you say?"

"I told him to watch how they treat women in this country. Maybe he'll learn something."

At 7:30 P.M. Bud finally left the hospital and drove home. On a school night, this usually meant he had thirty minutes to spend with the children before bed. That was on a good night. Usually they were too engrossed in a prime-time TV show, or he was wound too tight. The "family" in "family physician" referred to other families, not his own.

Bud turned into the winding lanes, cozy cul-de-sacs, and lush, private three-acre lots that made up Dunwoody Hills. Most of his neighbors were doctors, lawyers, and real estate agents he recognized by their cars. The one notable exception was Dean Martin, who lived at the end of Voss Drive. Martin headed the Neighborhood Watch program with a zeal that scared some of the older neighbors.

Bud rounded the last curve. His house was on the left, four down from the end of the block. With a sinking heart, he slowed down. On

. . . .

both sides of the road ahead, vans and media trucks were double-parked as far as the eye could see. Rarely were neighbors seen talking on their front lawns. Today they were out in full force. It didn't take Bud long to realize they were pointing at him, not waving, as he eased by in his Saab. A group of neighborhood skate-boarders reached out affectionately to touch the sides of his slow-moving car.

"Yes! Way to go! All right!" they called out behind him.

His seven-year-old executive brick home with its two-story foyer and dramatic windows was lit up like a Hollywood film location. The media crews had pooled light sources. Twenty or so reporters were queued up, waiting to stand in front of the house during their live remotes. TV news copters circled overhead.

"The Paynes must be crazy," he heard someone loudly call out.

Then the media crews converged on his car. Bud quietly inched forward behind closed windows as they called his name, fired questions, and aimed their videocams from all directions. When he reached the bottom of the driveway, he calmly activated the automatic garage door opener. The metal garage door closed behind him before any of the paparazzi could squeeze inside.

The reporters watched in disgust. Mrs. Payne wouldn't allow them on the property, so they waited. Talking and laughing loudly, roaming the street, smoking cigarettes and drinking coffee, and converging on passing motorists, they enjoyed their constitutional right to keep vigil all night beside the curb.

Inside the kitchen, Douglas and Lisa were ransacking the well-stocked cabinets for appetizers to offer their houseguests.

"Oxtail soup?" Douglas asked.

"Snails?" asked Lisa. "I know! Animal crackers!"

"Hello, is this Braxton's slaughterhouse?" Gail was talking on the cordless phone, moving restlessly around the kitchen like a field sergeant.

"I want to order twenty gallons of fresh cow blood. Yes, that's right. No, this isn't a prank call! I don't have to explain what it's for. It's personal."

As soon as she hung up, the phone rang. Gail shut off the ringer.

. . . .

In the background, the voice added its message to the dozens already on the answering machine.

"Dr. Payne, this is Michael Feder, Federhead Productions. Oprah Winfrey's people just called and told me about your story. I can't tell you how excited I am—I love this story and I love you people. I'm Fed-Exing a proposal for a Movie of the Week. Look it over. Call me."

Bud poked his head into the kitchen, half expecting to see tribesmen lounging by the kitchen island or the gas-microwave combo oven.

"Where's the tribe?" he asked softly.

Gail, Douglas, and Lisa turned toward him at the same time and fixed him with the same accusing stare.

"How could you?" Gail asked.

"Gail, you saw what happened. I had to get Hope to the hospital."

"Well, how is she?" Gail asked firmly.

"Fine."

"I still don't understand how you could invite the whole tribe to our house, Bud."

"What could I do? I couldn't just leave them at the airport. Not after they made me an honorary member of the tribe."

"Lisa's an honorary member of the Mickey Mouse Club. But that doesn't mean she can invite Mickey and his crew to spend the night at our house."

"Can I?" asked Lisa.

The doorbell chimed in the background.

"I'm sure it's been a little inconvenient," he said.

"A little inconvenient?! Do you have any idea what we've been through?" Gail pointed at the floor. "We've got more than twenty tribesmen with jet lag in our unfinished basement. And that's not all. We've got over thirty thousand dollars' worth of airline tickets charged to our gold card. I don't call that a little inconvenient, do you?"

Bud cleared his throat as the doorbell chimed again. "Thirty thousand dollars?"

"The legal department is checking into how it could've hap-

. . . .

pened. But the bottom line is—they said we're responsible unless they can prove a case of fraud."

"Gail, we can't have my tribe arrested for credit card fraud."

The doorbell chimed without stopping.

Gail nodded in the direction of the children. "We'll talk about it later. Can you get the door? That must be the pizza."

The pizza delivery boy, a long-haired teenager wearing untied mountain-climbing boots, was practically hidden behind the towering stack of pizza boxes. He followed Bud down the stairs leading to the unfinished basement.

At the bottom of the steps, plastic seashell-covered night lights glowed softly from the electrical outlets.

The warriors stood on one leg, still dusty with African soil, holding their spears, at the bottom of the steps. The elders, women, children, and the old woman and her goat rested peacefully on blankets next to unused cots.

Kimo and a few others spoke in low tones near the sliding glass doors.

The pizza boy stopped beside the warriors, then craned his neck up at them. "Cool, Dr. Payne! Why didn't you tell me you're hosting an Olympic team?"

"Bud!" Gail called out from the top of the stairs.

"So, who gets the steak and cheese?"

Hurrying up the steps, Bud found Gail pointing anxiously at the answering machine.

"Dr. Payne. Pick up the phone. I know you're in there." There was a long pause. "This is Dean Martin, Neighborhood Watch. I'm still waiting."

Bud answered the phone, "Hello, Dean? I know why you're calling."

"No kidding." Dean breathed heavily out his nose. Bud wondered what his alcohol count was. "Doctor, what's all the fuss about in front of your house?"

"You don't know?"

"If I knew, would I ask?"

. . . .

"Well, Dean . . ."

"Make it simple so I can understand. I didn't spend twenty years of my life in school, you know . . . Hold on."

Bud waited.

"Turn down the TV!" Dean screamed. "Go ahead, Dr. Payne."

"Well, Dean, we've got some celebrity house guests staying with us."

"Anybody I've heard of?"

"No, I doubt it. But the media won't leave them alone. I'm not sure how to get rid of them."

Long pause on the other end. "The house guests or the media?"

"The media," said Bud.

Dean Martin cleared his throat. "I'll handle it."

Thirty minutes later, a mosquito-control truck rumbled down the street towards the Payne's house. From the back of the truck spewed a thick, wet fog of pesticide. With much shouting and cursing, the journalists and camera crews collected their equipment and ran for cover inside their vans and trucks. When the truck stalled in front of the Paynes' house, clouding the street with noxious fumes, the reporters left for the night. Later, none of the neighbors thought it strange that the mosquito-control truck was parked outside Dean Martin's house until the wee hours.

Bud spoke over the portable phone as he walked down the basement steps. "Cynthia, how is she?"

"She's sleeping, Doctor. The nurses are in and out like you wouldn't believe."

"How late are you staying?"

"Another hour. I'll be back in the morning."

"Great," he said. "Can you talk to someone for me? We have Hope's family staying with us in our home. Could you ask them if they need anything?"

"Anything to help out."

Bud held out the phone to Kimo, who seemed unsure what to do with it. After Bud mimed a bit, pointing to his ear and mouth and

. . . .

the receiver and mouthpiece, respectively, Kimo grasped the phone. He held it a good distance away from his head.

"Go ahead," Bud called out to Cynthia. He overheard her speaking in Swahili. Kimo's face was expressionless, even as he handed the phone back to Bud.

Bud wearily climbed the stairs back to the main floor. "Thanks for trying," he said into the phone.

"Some Maasai can be ornery," Cynthia said. "My grandfather was Maasai. He used to say that no matter how much he scolded my grandmother, she never obeyed him. My grandfather died when I was still young. If he was still alive, I'd guess I'd have to take a stick to him."

FIFTEEN

In their king-size bed, Bud woke up to a foot pressed against his cheek. Douglas's foot.

Lisa stood next to the bed. She carried a tray of cereal, milk, and bowls. "Daddy, I thought the tribe would like breakfast. But they're gone."

"Good," said Gail dreamily.

"Lisa, they're sleeping," said Bud. He sat up in bed. "Remember how sleepy Mommy and I were when we flew back from Kenya?"

"Yes, I remember. But, Daddy . . . I looked everywhere."

"Did you call 911?" asked Douglas.

"Darling, it was very sweet of you to bring them breakfast." He eyed the green cereal designed after a popular Saturday morning cartoon character. "But they're very careful about what they eat."

"Where do you think they are, Daddy?" Lisa's voice was rising. The tray trembled in her small hands.

"Go look again. But quietly. Okay, dear?"

Bud closed his eyes as Lisa padded out of the room. A moment later they heard a loud scream.

"Daddy! Hurry!"

Bud and Gail threw off the covers together as they dashed out of the bedroom. Bud was three steps ahead of Gail when they reached the kitchen.

Lisa was pointing out the window over the sink. "There they are."

Bud stared out the window, then gripped the counter with both hands.

"Oh, my God!" said Gail.

Douglas walked in behind her carrying his Louisville Slugger bat for protection. "What is it?"

"Mud-plastered huts and a thorn fence," Bud gasped. "A Maasai settlement."

"In our backyard!" said Lisa.

Like a scene from the African plains, warriors and maidens finished weaving Gail's tulips, daffodils, roses, and shrubs into a thorn fence that surrounded seven huts. Women were busy slathering mud onto the last thatched frame while their children chased each other around their legs.

A young girl carried a bucket of water from the spring, actually a broken water pipe bubbling in the mud—the remains of the fountain were scattered under the tree. Thirty feet up, a warrior broke off branches and tossed them down to the children.

Elders caucused beside the fig tree where the goat chewed the last patch of remaining green sod.

"Whoa!" Douglas said. "Major relandscaping! They must've worked all night."

Gail fingered the top button of her gown. Six years of planning, hard work, and love were gone overnight.

"It's a natural disaster . . . Like a tornado hit it . . . A human tornado."

"I'm sorry, Gail," said Bud.

"Sorry, Mom," said Douglas and Lisa.

"I'll be okay. It's just quite a shock, that's all." She covered her hand over her mouth. "Oh, my God. I have to call the *Backyard Magazine.*" It was more than she could bear. She rushed out of the room.

Bud, Douglas, and Lisa slowly faced the window again.

Lisa was the first to speak. "I bet we're the only kids in our school with a village in their backyard."

"Duh. . . . Try the only kids in Western civilization," said Douglas.

. . . .

81

At that moment Bud's beeper went off. He checked the dial, then put his arms around his children. "Guys, I want you to stay home from school today to be with your mother. They're doing an important test on Hope this morning—I've got to be there. I'll be back as soon as I can."

SIXTEEN

Cynthia Goodman stroked Hope's hand while talking quietly with her mother in the radiology room. Pika held on to every word Cynthia shared with them. She recognized a lifeline when she saw one. Cynthia was going to save her daughter. Cynthia was family—she had Maasai blood.

Hope was the center of attention. She faced the wall as Dr. Rohrman, the cardiologist, leaned over her, aiming her long hypodermic.

Cynthia quietly explained the heart catheterization process to Pika and the laibon. "They put bright dye into her blood. The dye lets the doctors see her blood pump through her heart on TV."

A few minutes later, Hope's heart was displayed on the monitor over the bed, and Dr. Rohrman tuned into the silhouette of throbbing muscle.

To the laibon, these people were always staring at the moving picture boxes. The boxes were everywhere in the hospital. He wasn't sure whether they revealed dreams or demons, but their presence was irritating, like flies buzzing around one's eyes.

Bud entered the room quietly and stood beside the cardiologist.

The dye was entering the heart. Like a white express train, entering the tunnels of the heart, speeding up and over ramps, bridges, and switches.

"The blood is backing up there in the chamber," Dr. Rohrman said, pointing at the monitor.

"She definitely needs a new valve," said Dr. Chandler. He leaned against the back wall, keeping to himself.

The laibon muttered quietly to Cynthia, sliding his hand over his long, narrow skull.

"He wants to know if we can see her soul," Cynthia said.

"Tell him we can, but it's cost prohibitive," Dr. Chandler replied dryly.

"He says it's bad to look inside her body."

"Tell him this isn't hurting her at all," said Bud.

"He says we may cure her body. But he fears we may hurt her soul."

"Let's show Mr. Laibon exactly what's going on," said Chandler, opening his white lab coat to reveal, presto, a plastic model of the heart. Moments earlier the display model had rested on a pedestal on the bookshelf behind Chandler.

With nimble fingers, the heart surgeon expertly twisted, flipped, and rotated the hinged red and blue coded valves to the atria and ventricles.

"Here's what we have. A simple heart. No strings attached."

As Cynthia interpreted, the laibon and Hope's mother followed Dr. Chandler's hands carefully.

"Now, watch carefully. We open the mitral valve of the heart. And what do we see? The left ventricle. A good strong wall here. But not so good here. See these doors to the heart? Stuck. Blood doesn't flow in and out. This is Hope's heart."

Now the laibon understood completely. By fixing this plastic model, they would heal Opana.

Chandler flipped back the mitral valves. "We go in here and . . . Presto. Loosen up the doors. Voilà." Chandler handed the heart to the laibon, who reverently cupped his hands to receive it.

A spring on the plastic heart model flew loose.

"Oops," said Chandler, watching the heart suddenly fly apart, scattering into a dozen pieces on the floor.

. . . .

The laibon stepped back, shaking his baton furiously at Chandler. "He broke her heart!" he called out loudly in Swahili.

"It's okay," Cynthia said calmly in reply. "We have more."

"God help us! He broke her heart!" the laibon shouted, pointing at Chandler.

"What's wrong?" asked Bud.

"He thinks Dr. Chandler broke Hope's heart."

Chandler pulled a long face. "Are you serious?"

"Tell him this is only for show," said Bud. "Hope is fine. See for yourself."

Hope clutched the bedsheet, gasping for air. The laibon's words had the effect of a final judgment on her. She couldn't breathe.

"Let's get some oxygen," said Bud.

Chandler eyed the monitor blip. "It's just a little tachycardia— nothing to worry about."

Quickly reaching her side, Cynthia reassured her. "There, there. You're going to be all right, child. Cynthia isn't going to let anything happen."

Chandler kept his eye on the monitor until her heart rate evened out again. They could all breathe a little easier now.

Hope smiled weakly, then raised her hand and pointed. The laibon had just snapped the last piece of the plastic heart model back together. He cupped the model in his large hands, then blew gently across its red and blue surface, cooling off Hope's heart.

"How did he do that?" asked Chandler, impressed.

A few minutes later, as Cynthia and Bud wheeled Hope's portable bed into the corridor, Chandler watched a familiar shape approach.

"Surprise!" said Gloria, swinging a wicker picnic basket at her side as if she was walking down a Parisian runway. "It's such a beautiful day, Jerome, I thought we could eat lunch outside on the grass."

Chandler was practically speechless. "Never, ever surprise me while I'm at work."

"C'mon, Jerome. Lighten up. Your office told me this was all you had scheduled for this morning."

. . . .

"Yeah, lighten up," said Cynthia, coming to Gloria's aid. "A picnic sounds like a wonderful idea."

"It sounds great to me," added Bud.

"Besides, you can't get sushi in the hospital cafeteria," said Gloria.

"Sushi?" Chandler finally let up. "Well, maybe under the circumstances I can forgive you." He took the wicker basket from her arm.

Gloria smiled sweetly at the laibon, who was staring at her short hemline. "I brought extra if you care to join us."

"No way," said Chandler, shaking his head firmly. "No way in . . ."

Water sprinklers freshened the deep green lawn of the hospital landscaped grounds. Under the shade of a sprawling oak tree, Chandler rested his head in Gloria's lap, gazing up into her bosom. Gloria's fingers glistened with sushi as she teased Chandler's lips with each juicy morsel.

The laibon sat on the grass beside them, his legs crossed, an untouched plate of sushi next to him. He seemed more interested in the huge rawhide bone that Gloria's Pekingese dog licked and nibbled. The bone was like no other he'd ever seen. But whenever he tried to touch it, the little rat-dog snarled and shook its ribbons and nail-polished little paws at him.

After lunch, Chandler led the laibon on a shortcut through the Tully emergency room waiting area. As usual, Chandler walked with his eyes averted from the waiting room crowd of young mothers, wailing babies and toddlers, mud-splattered construction workers, diabetic and hypertensive elderly, and other specimens that filled the ER day and night.

A young doctor stopped in front of them. "Dr. Chandler, what do you think of this EKG?"

The laibon kept his eyes on a Korean woman, who rocked slowly in her seat, cradling her towel-wrapped arm to her chest. She waited patiently in the uncomfortable plastic chair under a buzzing fluorescent light. Her arm, seared with burning oil while frying eggrolls at the Lucky Star Restaurant the night before, was leaking brown pus

· · · ·

86

through the towel. Late last night, when she could no longer dice carrots, the family called a cab and sent her to Tully Hospital.

The cabdriver had told her to wait inside and that someone would help her. But she had been waiting for three hours. Still no one helped her. Then she saw the tall, black healer stroll in the doors. As soon as he saw how much pain she was in, he came straight over.

The laibon lifted the towel off the arm. When he blew on the burn, she clenched her teeth tightly. He took moist leaves from a pouch that he wore around his neck and placed them on her arm. When he blew on the arm this time, the woman relaxed. The mint was like a fresh breeze over her skin.

Chandler finished spooling through the EKG printout. "No signs of ischemia." He handed the paper back, then glanced around. The laibon was gone. But the mothers, toddlers, construction workers, and alcoholics waiting in the room were all staring in the same direction.

The laibon was kneeling in front of a smiling Korean woman. Reaching into his pouch, he grabbed a handful of mud and spread it over the burn. He finished the compound off with a sprinkling of small white feathers.

"I don't believe this," Chandler muttered.

Near the ER doors, an elderly security guard spoke into his portable phone. "We need Mr. Moorehead in the ER . . . ASAP."

A few minutes later, Richard burst through the double doors into the crowded ER. On a typical day, the crowd would have brought a smile to his lips. The ER was the hospital's biggest moneymaker. If it wasn't for the steady stream of traumatized gunshot victims and highway casualties, they'd be out of business in a week.

But today was different. As he worked his way through the crowd, he was joined by the security guard. Together they crossed over to the laibon and Chandler in time to see the laibon hold his hand, palm up, in front of the Korean woman.

She reached into her purse, but then saw the laibon point at the red necklace she was wearing. Without hesitating, she slipped the necklace off and placed it in his outstretched palm.

. . . .

Richard stared in disbelief at the mud and feathers. "What in God's name is this? Dr. Chandler, did you authorize this treatment?"

"What do you think?"

"I think we have a witch doctor performing unauthorized care in our hospital. I think we're in deep voodoo." He reached into his coat pocket, found a coupon, and handed it to the Korean woman.

"Madam, I'm terribly sorry about this. This is good for a free trip to the salad bar in the cafeteria. It's good for one adult."

Richard gestured for an orderly to lead the smiling Korean woman away.

"All right," said Chandler. "I'll take him back to Dr. Payne now."

"I don't think so." Richard turned to the security guard. "Take our medicine man to my office. I'll need to make a full report."

"All right, you heard the man." The guard jerked his thumb at the laibon. "Let's go."

The laibon raised his rhino-horn baton in his hand as if he expected trouble.

"Take it easy, old fella."

Richard was getting impatient. "Here, I'll take one arm, you take the other. On a count of three . . ."

"I wouldn't do that," said Chandler.

"One . . . two . . ."

Richard stopped counting. The laibon lowered his rhino horn to within a few inches from Richard's gabardine trousers. Slowly circling the crotch area with the polished, gleaming baton, the laibon began chanting. The oloiboni had warned him in advance, his enemy would be one with hair red like flames. Thus he came prepared to put out the fire.

Rolling his eyes, Richard was acutely aware of the curious crowd of families and hospital staff gathered around him. "That's enough," he finally said. He finished the count. "Three."

The laibon tapped the baton three times in rapid succession. Suddenly, a poof of yellowish smoke rose from Richard's crotch.

The guard backed off, covering his pubic area with his hands.

. . . .

88

Richard waved the sulphuric smoke away from his pants, which were stained with yellow powder. In a tightly controlled voice, pointing at the double doors, he said to the laibon, "You and I are going to have a nice long chat with Dr. Payne."

"I don't want to see him in this hospital again. As far as I'm concerned, he's lost his privileges." Richard tapped a pencil against his teeth. He leaned back in his leather swivel seat behind his desk.

"Let's be reasonable," said Bud. "We've only got a few more days before the child is ready for surgery. She needs him here."

"Look, if anyone is to blame, it's me," Chandler said. "I let him out of my sight."

Bud glanced at Chandler. Maybe there was hope for the cold-hearted surgeon after all.

"Unfortunately, hospital administrators can't afford to be as noble and forgiving as doctors." Richard pointed at the laibon. "He's out of here. That's final."

Richard stood up, smoothed down the front of his trousers, frowning at the faded yellow stain which he had tried unsuccessfully to wash out.

"Oh, by the way. Ask him what did he mean by that little performance in the ER? He ruined a two-hundred-dollar pair of slacks."

Cynthia asked the laibon in Swahili. She listened carefully to his reply, once clucking her tongue at him when he said the administrator smelled as sweet as a stomach wound.

At the end, she addressed Richard. "He says you and your warrior were going to attack him. So he took away your privileges . . ."

She tried to translate the next part with a straight face, but it wasn't easy. "He placed a hex on your manhood. He says your thingamajig will shrivel like grass without rain, then break off and scatter in the wind."

Bud, Chandler, and Cynthia bit their tongues, trying hard not to smile.

"Voodoo?" Richard said shrilly. "A hex on my manhood? Thank you very much, Dr. Payne, for this lovely multicultural experience!"

. . . .

At the curb outside the hospital, Bud leaned into the cabdriver's window. The laibon sat in the rear of the cab.

"Take him to 951 Voss Drive. Then escort him to my backyard, where his family is staying." He handed the driver a twenty. "This should cover it."

Minutes later, they were bogged down in the middle of downtown traffic. The cabdriver leaned on his horn. "It's backed up clear to the civic center," he said over his shoulder. No reply.

When he checked out the backseat, all he saw was the open door. The dude with the long ears and wearing a blanket was marching down the center lane. "Hey, where are you going? Come back here!"

The laibon tightened his blanket around his shoulders. Carrying his rhino-horn baton at his side, he strode purposefully down the congested avenue.

SEVENTEEN

Gail sat at the kitchen table slowly thumbing through a scrapbook of photos. One page showed the Payne family, wearing their Easter finery, posing among the lilies in the dazzling backyard. She forced herself to acknowledge that there would be no Easter lilies this year. No cavalcade of tulips and daffodils. No magazine stories on her backyard unless the *National Enquirer* heard about it.

Gail reached for the phone by her hand, then rehearsed what she was going to say. "Hello, *Backyard Magazine*? This is Gail Payne. Can we reschedule this afternoon? How about in . . . four years?"

The clothes dryer in the corner emitted a loud angry buzz. Crossing the kitchen, she glanced out the window, once again confirming her worst fear. However, this time she saw something new.

Douglas nudged Lisa inside the entrance to the thorn fence, then followed his little sister a few steps behind. At the same moment, three warriors came out wearing headdresses, and carrying shields and long-bladed spears.

Gail wasted no time. She hurried through the backyard, oblivious to the wreckage. She didn't slow down until she reached the thorn fence. Then she caught her breath, glancing away from the tulips, daffodils, and white roses that were artfully woven into the twisted branches and thorns.

"Douglas? Lisa?"

"We're in here, Mom!"

Gail stepped inside the thorn fence, prepared for anything.

Douglas and Lisa sat cross-legged on the ground with their new best friends. Two Maasai boys were playing mbau, an ancient version of checkers, while the other children watched. Two rows of small slots were dug into the dirt, so that the playing area resembled an open egg carton. One of the boys quickly moved a handful of pebbles around the slots, dropping one into each slot.

"Is everything okay?" Gail asked.

"Yeah," said Douglas. "Look at this cool game, Mom. All you need to play it are some stones and the ground."

Lisa held up a tiny brown doll. "And they know how to make dolls out of sticks and clay!"

In the background, the mothers were putting the finishing design touches on huts, carrying bundles of sticks, and nursing babies. Life had already settled into a normal routine for the Backyard Tribe.

A familiar voice called out, "Isn't it magical!"

Fanny stepped out of her hut. Her head was shaved just like the rest of the Maasai females' and she wore beaded earrings, necklaces, and a calfskin dress. Tall and slender, she could have been a pale cousin of the backyard tribe.

"Fanny, what happened?"

"It's Fanno," she corrected Gail. "What do you think?" She spun around like a model on the runway. Several elders watched her from afar.

"I don't know what to think," said Gail.

"I know how you feel. Yesterday we confused our numb suburban existence with being alive. Today we're running on all six senses."

"Fanny . . . Fanno," Gail said gently. "Have you talked to anyone about your new lifestyle?"

"No." Fanny made a sweeping gesture at the newly landscaped backyard. "Have you?"

"There hasn't been time," Gail replied. "Bertram doesn't know?"

"Bertram doesn't know squat, dear. That man refers to chiropractors as 'those damn witch doctors.' He still swears by the four food groups. Any meal served without meat is an in-between snack to

. . . .

him. Right now he's in Scotland trying to hit a little white ball into a tiny hole in the ground."

A friendly Maasai woman put a beaded necklace around Gail's neck.

"Thank you," said Gail.

"Gail, do you realize what's happened back here?"

Gail nodded grimly.

"Your backyard might become the spiritual center of a new age. Imagine villages springing up in backyards across America. You must be so proud of them and what they've done!"

Gail smiled at the friendly Maasai women gathered around her. She tried to be as diplomatic as possible.

"Well, I will say that only a well-run family could've done this. Our family has problems just taking long car trips together."

A well-dressed woman appeared at the opening of the thorn fence. Her blue-tinted hair was the same light shade as Gail's hydrangeas.

"Hello, Mrs. Payne? Did we catch you on a bad day?" she said, glancing through her bifocals at the ravaged backyard, then at Gail.

"Can I help you?" Gail asked uneasily.

"Mrs. Laplace? The *Backyard Magazine*?"

Gail swallowed heavily. Following a few steps behind Mrs. Laplace was a short, huffing and puffing photographer loaded down with cameras and equipment bags.

"Oh, no," said Gail. "I was just going to pick up the phone and call you."

The photographer dropped his equipment bags, lowered his Ray-Bans, and scanned the mud-plastered huts. "Is someone pulling my leg?" He turned to Mrs. Laplace. "Or did you slip something naughty into my milk at the restaurant?"

"Mrs. Payne! On the double!"

Gail recognized Dean Martin's voice over the public address system, which he used quite liberally on his patrol golf cart.

"Excuse me," Gail told her guests. "Feel free to look around."

Dean Martin and dog, a drooling mixed breed who sat

. . . .

93

straighter and taller than Dean, were waiting beside the Paynes' garage.

"Mrs. Emmons called me. Three Zulu warriors just cut through her yard space."

"They're Maasai. Not Zulu," said Gail, out of breath.

"I don't give a flying flick who they are. They're armed to the teeth—and I don't think they're looking for a lawn job, do you?"

"No." Gail just stared at him.

"I'll find them." Dean gunned the golf cart motor. "It's about time we nipped this in the bud."

"I'll call Bud," Gail murmured in a daze.

The three Maasai warriors stood motionless in the terraced backyard a few blocks away from the Paynes' house. The afternoon sun glinted off the long steel blades of their spears. In their other hands, they gripped the handles of their buffalo-hide shields. Beneath their towering ostrich-feather and lion-mane headdresses, their faces were expressionless as they watched the swimmer splash furiously back and forth in his single-lap pool.

Ten minutes later they caused quite a stir at little Carol Martin's sixth birthday party. Her little friends stood with gaping mouths as blond-haired Carol, blindfolded and staggering forward with the donkey tail, headed straight toward the warriors, who stood by the hedge watching the party in fascination.

After that, the warriors continued to forge ahead through the subdivision until they reached a hill. In the distance, a long clearing sloped toward a white-columned mansion. From the ridge, they enjoyed a view of the ten or so dairy cows grazing in the lush grass.

A sign on the rail fence read HAWK FARM, HOME OF BABS THE COW.

As soon as Bud heard Gail's out-of-breath message, he canceled the rest of his appointments and rushed out of the office.

Now he was cruising the subdivision in search of his honorary tribesmen. Visitors often managed to get lost in the maze of cul-de-sacs and circular roads. For security, there was only one road in and out. Once, an elderly Polish man had wandered away from his

· · · ·

daughter's house and wasn't found until the next morning, dehydrated, lying under a mimosa tree only two blocks away.

Bud pulled up beside a county road maintenance crew. Three guys stood around and watched one other guy tear up the road with a jackhammer.

"Excuse me," said Bud. "Have you seen any tall young men with long hair, red togas, and carrying spears and shields?"

Their derogatory answer rang in Bud's ear as he followed a dirt road on the outskirts of the subdivision. In the distance, he saw a golf cart on the hill overlooking the pasture. Dean Martin and his dog were silhouetted at the top.

As Bud scrambled up the hill, Dean lifted a Budweiser out of an ice chest and popped the tab.

"I feel sorry for you, Payne."

"Why? What's wrong?"

He guzzled half the beer. "You know who Jimmy Hawk is?"

"The old farmer?"

"Yeah. He used to own all this land. But each time he had to sell another forty acres to a pencil-necked developer, he got a little meaner." Dean pointed at the flattened rail fence and the empty pasture. "He loved those cows more than anything."

"Loved?" Bud asked weakly.

"Loved. Your house guests just rustled Jimmy Hawk's cows. And Jimmy's from the old school."

"Which school is that?"

"The kind that shoots first, hires lawyers later."

Carol the Birthday Girl was bobbing for apples when the warriors herded the cows past her birthday party.

Farther on, the lap swimmer had just completed his hundredth lap. He still wore his blue, fogged-up goggles, and was leaning against the side of the pool, when he made out the vague shape of someone—his girlfriend—by the pool.

"Chris, would you hand me the towel?" he asked, pointing to the back of a nearby chair.

The warrior picked up the towel off the chair with the end of his

. . . .

spear and handed it to him. Cows drank thirstily at both ends of the pool.

"Thanks, babe," he responded, without removing his fogged-up goggles.

EIGHTEEN

After Bud parked the Saab in the driveway, he dashed around the garage, where he barely avoided a head-on collision with a blue-haired society woman followed by a short, excited photographer, who walked backward, snapping a final roll of photographs.

"In all my years, I've never seen anything like it," said Mrs. Laplace, hurrying out.

"Tell me about it," said the photographer.

Then Bud saw what they were talking about.

Two warriors gripped the sides of the cow as the third grasped the head, smothering its face with the ceremonial calfskin.

The cow slumped to the ground.

"No!" Bud called out.

The tribe enthusiastically waved back to him.

Gail came to the kitchen window and saw the cows milling outside the thorn fence. The tribe stood around the fresh beef, blocking her view.

"Bud, where did those cows come from?" she called out.

"Jimmy Hawk's."

"That was nice of him. I thought his cows were just for show."

"We're still working out the details," Bud said guiltily.

"Is Babs down there?"

"Who?"

· · · ·

"You know, Babs. She used to star in all those milk commercials. Each year Jimmy invites the area schoolchildren to visit Babs at the farm."

Mingling with the tribe outside the thorn fence, Douglas and Lisa watched as a Maasai elder knelt beside the cow and sliced into its belly with his razor-sharp knife.

Bud stepped up behind them and put his hands on their shoulders. "Are you kids okay," he asked.

"Dad, they killed Babs," said Douglas.

"She went fast, Dad," Lisa added.

"Bud, it's all right," said Fanny, standing beside the children. "I told the kids how the Maasai believe that all the cows on earth belong to them. That's why they feel justified in repossessing these cows."

Bud stared at Fanny's shaved head, necklaces, and calfskin dress. "Fanny, what happened to you?"

"It's Fanno." She fiddled with her dangling earrings—she had decided at the last minute to forgo the elongated earlobes. "You wouldn't happen to know if the laibon is dropping by tonight, would you?"

"I don't know." He searched her green eyes. "Why?"

"Don't be jealous, Dr. Payne. You Western doctors don't have all the answers, you know."

"Fanny . . . Fanno, I don't understand."

"Of course not," she said as she turned on her heels and entered the thorn fence.

Bud saw that the tribe had prepared a huge bonfire to roast their meat over. A few backyards over, he could see the Leons grilling steaks in their brick barbecue pit. It was a perfect evening for a cookout. He pulled himself together. He had work to do. "Kids, you better go in now. Tell your mother I'm going to be late for dinner. I'll be at Jimmy Hawk's."

"Good luck, Dad," said Douglas.

From the top step of Jimmy Hawk's mansion, Bud had an excellent view of what remained of Jimmy's wooded pastures and what had

· · · ·

replaced them—energy-efficient homes, three-car garages, and cul-de-sacs.

Bud felt a twinge of guilt. The stolen cattle were one strike against him. The subdivision was another. He tried to remember why he and Gail had moved there. The house was spacious, the neighborhood friendly and secure, good access to the hospital, good local schools ... Before, they'd always lived in old, romantic houses. Wonderful Victorian homes teeming with history and bugs, humidity, faulty wiring and leaking plumbing. After Douglas was born, the romance shot out the old, noninsulated windows. So Bud and Gail had searched for modern housing. Like pioneers of old, they faced almost insurmountable odds. Misleading ads, unscrupulous real estate agents, banking deals gone awry. Finally, after many trials and tribulations, and with great weariness, they had settled in the subdivision.

Bud lifted the heavy door knocker. He doubted if Jimmy Hawk would be interested in the story of how the Paynes came to settle on his back forty.

Thud. Moments later he heard cowboy boots across the marbled foyer. The front door opened.

Bud had never seen Jimmy Hawk up close before. He'd passed him in his pickup a few times. In person, Jimmy seemed much bigger, older, and meaner. Rawboned from his jaw to his knuckles, he seemed quite capable of dropping down and giving you a hundred one-arm pushups. Over one denim-shirt shoulder, he wore a coil of rope.

"Good evening. Are you Mr. Hawk?"

"Who wants to know?"

"I'm Dr. Payne. We need to talk."

"Dr. Payne? What kind of name is that for a doctor? You one of those door-to-door chiropractors?"

"No, I'm a family physician. I live nearby."

"Well, I don't need any. And unless you're here because my cows didn't show up for dinner, you can kiss my hairy butt good night."

"Actually, that's what we need to talk about."

. . . .

Tension poured into Jimmy Hawk's jaw like hot lava. "Start talking, boy."

"A few hours ago, warriors from a tribe of seminomadic herdsmen living in my backyard repossessed your cows."

"What in hell's bells . . ."

"It's part of their cultural heritage. See, the Maasai believe that God gave them all the cows on earth. So, when they saw your cows . . . well, you know what happened next."

Jimmy started grinning, slow and ugly. "Where are the cameras?" He glanced around for the hidden cameras.

"This isn't a joke. Your cows are in my backyard."

"In your backyard?" Jimmy asked, still going along. "Isn't that nice."

"All but one."

"Which one might that be?"

"Babs. The warriors suffocated her in a ceremonial ritual. I'm sorry."

"Seminomadic warriors suffocated Babs?" His smile went south. "What kind of sick joke is this? Did my ex-wife send you?"

"It's no joke."

Jimmy gripped the rope over his shoulder. "Then somebody is going to pay."

Bud's Reebok tennis shoes matched Jimmy's crusty cowboy boots stride for stride as they walked toward the showdown in the back-yard village.

At the thorn fence entrance, three warriors suddenly blocked their entrance with their buffalo-hide shields. Jimmy stared incredulously at the shields and the long, razor-sharp blades in the hands of the tall, lithe warriors. When the warriors saw Bud, they smiled in recognition, lowered their shields and let them pass. Inside the thorn fence, sparks from the blazing bonfire showered the air. Children chased each other merrily around the fire. The bones of the barbecued cow were strewn about the smooth dirt. Babs's bones.

Kimo nodded greetings at Bud, then stared long and hard at Jimmy.

. . . .

"Tell him I want my cows back," Jimmy told Bud, never taking his eyes off Kimo. "Now."

Bud pointed at the cows, who wandered freely behind the thorn fence under the watchful eyes of the elders. "Cows." Then he pointed up at Jimmy. "His."

"Hellfire, Payne . . . I could've done that myself! You can't even speak their lingo?"

"Sorry, Hawk. But Swahili wasn't a language option in medical school."

Jimmy was still shaking his head as he approached his cattle. Four elders stood beside the cows, affectionately feeding them grass out of their hands. One of the elders gestured for Jimmy to approach. When he reluctantly complied, the Maasai elder grabbed Jimmy's hand and placed it under the cow. Bud moved in quickly to prevent a brawl.

Jimmy's anger melted as he stripped off his glove and touched the spot near the udder again.

"Well bless my britches if that's not the damndest thing I've ever seen. It's a lymph gland infection" Jimmy shook his head in disbelief. "I've taken Babbette, Bab's oldest daughter, to two veterinary specialists and all the way to the state university and no one could tell me what's wrong."

Jimmy held out his hand in thanks to the Maasai elder. His smile faded quickly as the ancient cattleman spit in his palm and then gripped Jimmy's hand firmly.

"You say they're cattle herders?" Jimmy asked Bud.

"The best."

"Anybody who can drive my cows across two miles of subdivision has got to be good."

Jimmy toed the dirt with the tip of his cowboy boot. Then he looked over and saw Fanno chewing on a blackened rib. His face suddenly darkened.

"I'm really sorry about Babs, Jimmy."

"Well, Babs was a good old girl. But she had a bad heart. I was going to have to put her down. It's better she went out in a blaze of

. . . .

glory." He wiped his good eye. "So what the hell are these people doing in your backyard?"

"It's a long story."

An hour later, Bud and Jimmy left the village under a chorus of waves from the elders, women, and children. Jimmy gnawed the last bit of meat off a rib.

"You know, they remind me of folks I knew when I was growing up. We used to call them old-fashioned. They were proud people. They took care of their own. They weren't full of crap like you and your neighbors.

"I roamed every inch of this land when I was a kid. You couldn't go a hundred feet without seeing a deer, raccoon, possum, snake, or some damn thing. Now look at it. The only living things for miles around are frozen in front of the boob tube like possums staring into the headlights of an oncoming sixteen-wheeler. Give me seminomadic herdsmen any day," Jimmy concluded.

Bud let the stinging comments slide. He was beginning to admire the old cowboy who could roll with the kind of punch the Maasai had just given him, then come up swinging against modern suburbia.

"You're going to let them keep the cows?"

"I'll lease them to you at market value. But you owe me fifteen thousand for Babs."

"Fifteen thousand? For a cow with a heart ailment?"

"Fifteen thousand, Payne." Jimmy tossed the bone aside. "Now you know why people don't barbecue blue-ribbon dairy cows."

It was almost midnight when Bud slipped under the bed covers next to Gail. She was propped up with pillows, reading *Road & Track* magazine. Stuffing a few pillows behind his head, Bud reached for the latest issue of the *AMA Journal* off his nightstand.

For a long time, neither of them turned a page.

"What a day," Gail said finally, laying her magazine down in her lap.

"*Road & Track?*" asked Bud as he retired his journal.

· · · ·

"I bought it to send to Sister Beth. It's nice. It has nothing about gardens in it."

"That reminds me, Gail. Was that the *Backyard Magazine* people I saw leaving today?"

"How fast were they moving?"

"They were flying."

"That was them."

"I'm sorry," he said, touching her hand.

"I've never been so embarrassed in my life. You should've seen their faces." She started giggling involuntarily.

"Are you okay?" Bud asked.

"Yes . . . They were so disoriented! Imagine walking into our backyard and expecting to see thousands of tulips and daffodils and"—she was laughing so hard she had to catch her breath—"and stepping into a scene straight out of 'Twilight Zone' meets 'National Geographic.' "

Bud laughed along with her. "You should've seen Jimmy Hawk's face when he went head-on with three warriors at the thorn fence."

"I bet our neighbors think we've lost our minds."

"Like Fanny," Bud chipped in.

Gail corrected him. "It's Fanno!"

Still laughing, they turned off the light and snuggled in together.

· · · ·

NINETEEN

Bud saw patients all morning. He was now forty minutes into his examination of Mrs. Eugenia Gaines, mother of six.
Bud allocated fifteen minutes per patient—but it had taken that long
to get past Mrs. Gaines' fear of a private exam. Since this was the
first time he had seen Mrs. Gaines without a child clinging to her
breast, he knew it must be serious.

"I don't know, Dr. Payne. I'm just feeling run down, and poor-
like, you know. That's not like me. Anybody will tell you that. I'm
aching all over."

"Where did it start?" Bud asked.

"I honestly don't know. The children keep me running from
morning till night, you know."

"Yes, ma'am."

"Maybe I just need some rest."

"Mrs. Gaines, I'd feel a whole lot better if we ran some tests," Bud
said. "We can't have you getting sick with all those children to take
care of."

"Ain't that the truth."

Afterward, Bud walked over to Tully Hospital to make the
rounds on his hospitalized patients.

For forty minutes of his time, a cardiac surgeon might be paid
three thousand dollars. Bud, a family physician, was looking at

. . . .

thirty. Richard Moorehead had a name for doctors like Bud—bottom feeders. No one could deny their importance in the food chain; they sucked up scum and kept the water clear for the beautiful angelfish, sharks, and porpoises—the surgeons, radiologists, and anesthesiologists—at the top.

Medical school reinforced the image. Surgeons like Dr. Chandler were exciting, charming, and brilliant role models leading interns into the dazzling world of high-tech surgery. Of course, ten years later when they were doing the same high-tech procedure for the thousandth time, it was a different story.

Great family physicians were more like your friendly aunt or uncle at the family reunion. Their concerns appeared more mundane, although they were in the front lines and had to diagnose all illnesses, which ranged from the simple to the sublime. Such as Mrs. Gaines' fatigue. Bud hoped the tests would prove all she needed was rest, but he suspected that she had something deadlier lurking in her. This uneasiness, this suspicion that each patient he routinely saw was being stalked by bigger, deadlier conditions, was the baggage Bud carried from day to day.

Hope held the palm-size microcassette recorder in her hand. She gave Bud and Cynthia a big smile, then pressed the Play button.

" 'Humpty Dumpty sat on a wall. Humpty Dumpty had a great fall. All the king's horses, and all the king's men, couldn't put Humpty together again.' "

Bud applauded Hope. She spoke English with a soft, lilting voice, but with precise enunciation. "That's incredible!" He turned to Cynthia. "I'm impressed by both of you."

"She's incredible, Dr. Payne." Cynthia beamed at her young patient. "She learns everything the first time around."

Hope beamed as she turned up the volume louder and louder, proudly playing one nursery rhyme after another.

"You're doing a wonderful job here."

"Thanks," said Cynthia, speaking louder to be heard over the tape recorder. "There is one thing, however. She misses the laibon. How's he doing?"

. . . .

"Uh-oh. I haven't seen him since he left the hospital yesterday."

"Any chance of him visiting before she goes into surgery?"

The nurse stopped jotting down notes on Hope's chart beside the bed. "No way. Not after what he did to the administrator."

"How did you hear about that?" Bud asked her.

"Are you kidding? You can't keep a thing like that—or lack thereof—a secret," she giggled.

Cynthia confirmed the nurse's statement. "The whole hospital's talking about the incredible shrinking man."

"I hope no one is taking that hex thing seriously," said Bud.

Richard saw it right away. Someone had drawn a Ken doll and written RICHARD MOOREHEAD beneath it in tiny block letters on a tile over the men's urinal.

He hummed to himself as he stood there doing his business. Let the staff have their fun, he thought. He knew the rumor mill was working overtime on the incident between him and the witch doctor. If ridiculing him lightened their steps, improved their morale, distracted them from their high car payments, then so be it.

However, the simple truth of the matter was that Richard Moorehead didn't have a superstitious bone in his body.

It was Richard Moorehead, for pete's sake, who tried to persuade the building committee to keep the thirteenth floor in the new hospital wing. "My God! What does that say about the world of modern medicine," he argued, "when we can't number a thirteenth floor because of some ancient superstition?" Of course, he bowed to popular pressure. Most patients would balk at receiving medical attention on a thirteenth floor. Also, as the architect reminded him, by skipping the thirteenth floor on a twenty-floor building, you got credit for having an extra story.

The men's room door opened. Two young orderlies entered at the same time and stopped laughing hilariously when they saw who was standing at the urinal. He was about finished as they stepped up to the wall on either side of him. As they faced the porcelain, both orderlies simultaneously glanced down at him.

No one said anything for a moment.

. . . .

"Satisfied?" Richard said, zipping up.

"Excuse me?" said the orderly on his right.

Once a week, or so it seemed, Western scientists discovered yet another ancient folk medicine that was medically sound. Was it so farfetched that a tribal healer, relying on thousands of years of trial and error, had developed a surefire way for shrinking a man's thingamajig?

"I asked if you were satisfied?"

The two orderlies swapped bewildered expressions behind Richard's back. "I don't know what you mean."

Richard stepped back, narrowing his eyes at both men. "You tell anyone what you just saw and you'll never work in this town again."

The laibon walked briskly through a landscape of towering glass and steel boxes that scraped the evening sky, dirtied as it was with the smoke that bellowed from the tails of buses and trucks.

He stopped to examine a flattened animal carcass beside the road. It was dry, stiff like bark. He held it up, turned it around in his hands. A few salvageable parts. Not much. A tongue and an earbone. Working deftly with his hands, he ignored the building people who gathered across the road to watch.

Most of the nomads he passed in the city ignored him. Some argued in loud, angry voices with the spirits of ancestors. Some wrestled with demons as they walked, occasionally stopping to kick and slash the air around them. Others poked quietly through trash cans, unwrapping food, and drinking whatever liquids they could find. When the laibon approached lost children and women who needed help, he would stop in front of them and wave his rhino-horn baton, the symbol of his healing powers. But they always drew back, afraid, refusing his attention.

Later, hearing the frenzied barking of wild dogs, he knew from experience the pack had gathered the courage to attack a weaker animal. The sound of the wild dogs gladdened his heart. No matter where you travel on earth, it is the same earth. No matter how many different tribes you meet, there is only one Maasai. He thanked God once again for making him Maasai.

. . . .

He took longer strides now, his blanket whipping across his legs. Between two buildings was a darkened space wide enough for a elephant to enter. In the dark alley, the dogs had cornered their prey. The nomad, a man in the middle years, was huddled over, protecting his vital organs and his head.

The laibon never slowed down as he entered the alley. As a pack, he knew the dogs were fearless. So he quickly sought out the leader, a lean animal with fangs bared like a starving hyena.

The Doberman's eyes met the laibon's. With a snarl that echoed loudly in the alley, he launched himself at the laibon's throat. Boom! Seventy pounds of teeth and muscle slammed against the wall and went down with a shudder. The laibon wiped the rhino-horn baton on his blanket. The o-rinka had many uses.

The pack of dogs raced past him, running out of the alley at a fast clip with the Doberman in the rear.

The laibon leaned over the dog's victim. The man was breathing in short, jerky breaths. His head was cold. His face, arms, and legs were bloody. Fortunately, his heavy, faded green jacket protected his vital organs. The laibon did the best he could with the herbs in his leather pouch. Crushing herbs in his hand, he moistened them with saliva, then held the compound under the man's nose. The man sneezed. His eyelids opened enough to permit a brief, incredulous glance at the Maasai laibon tending his wounds. Then he fell back unconscious.

After applying salve to the wounds on the man's face and scalp, the laibon slung the stranger over his shoulder. He was heavy, much heavier than any warrior he'd ever carried back from battle. Slowly he followed the trail of wires back to the hospital. He had memorized the trail, because he knew the wires would lead him back to Opana.

Things were quiet in the emergency room. It was a warm, weekday night—no high school football games, no gas heaters roaring away in flimsy house trailers. The kind of night where the ER security guard had time to savor each fresh, unfortunate accident victim, and reflect on victims past. Like the guy who rushed in claiming he'd swallowed a live gerbil (X rays proved later that he hadn't). Or like the hospital administrator. Talk about your worst nightmares!

The guard's daydreams were suddenly interrupted with a whoosh of the automatic doors.

The laibon carried the bleeding, unconscious man in over his shoulder. At once, three orderlies came running. They loaded the wounded man on a gurney, and wheeled him away.

The guard backed away from the laibon. As he did, he covered his crotch with his portable phone. "Uh, thanks for bringing him," he stammered. "But I can't let you stay."

Across the waiting room, Chandler stepped out of the elevator and saw the laibon near the ER doors. He quickened his step.

"What's going on?" Chandler asked.

"He just dropped off some guy in serious condition. But I can't let him stay. He's on the most wanted list." He pointed to his clipboard, not expecting the hard-nosed cardiac surgeon to pay attention to his problems.

"What are you going to do?" asked Chandler.

"What do you suggest?" the guard asked, surprised.

Chandler hesitated for a moment, checked his watch, then motioned to the laibon. "C'mon. Let's go."

Chandler cruised along in the Porsche. On the CD player, Marcus Roberts was playing a Thelonious Monk tune. Traffic was light. He glanced over at the laibon seated beside him.

The weary laibon was sitting low in the leather bucket seat. As the cityscape of lighted plazas, architectural wonders, and sidewalk cafes zipped by him, he didn't raise an eyebrow.

After driving in silence for a few minutes, Chandler reached out and turned down the volume. "Let me get something off my chest. I know you're not impressed by us. Or me. But we do a good job of treating a lot of people. Unfortunately, our system isn't designed for taking care of one person at a time like yours. That's too bad, but that's the way it is."

Chandler paused, almost surprising himself by sharing private

· · · ·

thoughts like this. "I don't usually open up to people like this. But, since you don't understand a word I'm saying, I guess it's okay."

The laibon leaned forward in his seat, then reached out with his hand, touching the CD volume switch, and gently turned up the music. Satisfied, he leaned back in the soft leather seat.

The laibon stopped in the backyard and sniffed the heavy smells of roasting meat in the air. Moments later, he was engulfed by hugs and handshakes as the warriors, followed by the other elders, women, and children rushed out to greet him.

In front of the bonfire, he drank deeply from the calabash. Then he bit into a piece of the bull's oozing liver—saved especially for him.

Among his most ardent admirers was the woman who seemed to have joined their tribe in his absence. Her name was Fanno. The laibon observed how she followed his every movement, smiling and winking at him whenever he glanced her way. In her green eyes, he saw spirits and demons struggling.

After eating, the laibon began a long speech concerning Opana's treatment. He told his people about the dream boxes the whites consulted at every opportunity. How the doctor had broken Opana's heart—but how with his own hands the laibon had fitted the pieces back together and blown life back into the heart.

He told them he could not foresee the outcome of the whites' medicine. He knew that you cannot treat a cruel condition with an easy cure. But he saw that Opana was dangling between their world and that of their dead ancestors.

He told them how he shrank the leg-that-does-not-walk of the hospital leader who tried to take him prisoner. He finished with a long story about a land without trees, grass, or sun, where wild dogs attacked nomads.

In their turn, the warriors spoke of wonders they had seen. Of the hairy man who swam in a trough, back and forth, unable to get out. Of the man watering his automobile as if it were alive. Of men and women who wrapped grass and leaves in large bags to give as gifts

. . . .

to men driving trucks. Of close-cropped grassy plains where men strolled with spears and hit balls into the wind. Each time, the men shouted the same short word "Fore" to scare the birds into the air. And they never killed a single thing!

TWENTY

Over the next two days, it was a rare moment when Hope and her mother weren't posing beside some politician, VIP, or various other civic leader for a photo op that would later appear on some handout, annual report, or social page.

Journalists from around the world flocked to the room. Hard-nosed skeptics outside the room, the correspondents softened like butter in the afternoon sun after five minutes with Hope. One reporter traveled all the way from Sydney, Australia, interviewed Hope for fifteen minutes, then turned around and flew straight back.

Politicians wallowed about the room like hippos, basking in the light of flashbulbs. When a former klansman-turned-congressman barged in for a quick, run-and-gun photo op, Cynthia adopted a fiercer visitation policy. No sooner did she see the ex-Klansman than she stomped on his Florsheims, gripped the back of his coat collar, and heaved him out of the room.

In addition to becoming Hope's bouncer, Cynthia became her spokesperson and chief operating officer. She no longer accepted stuffed animals, or variations on the fifteen-dollar flower display. Now Cynthia requested donations for Hope Chest, Inc., a nonprofit organization sponsoring emergency surgery for needy children.

Hope Chest, Inc., was founded after a very short conversation between Hope and Cynthia.

"How many other children have you and Dr. Payne helped?" Hope asked Cynthia one morning.

"Just you, Hopeful. You're the first and only."

"Why?"

Cynthia couldn't think of a good answer to that. Thus, Hope Chest, Inc.

Bud loved the idea. He immediately contacted a lawyer who volunteered to draw up the incorporation papers. The hospital gift shop was already making plans for Hope Chest T-shirts and caps.

Early in the morning, before official visiting hours, Hope visited children in the intensive care unit. She set off a wave of excitement when she arrived. The nurses watched in awe as Hope, reciting nursery rhymes, slowly walked down the hall and visited with each ICU kid. Hope's smiles and little touches were becoming the most valuable, unbillable resource in the hospital.

In the newspaper, TV, and radio news reports, Bud insisted that the Maasai village was strictly off limits to the public. Privately, he arranged visits by a few special groups.

On Sunday afternoon, the congregation of his receptionist's Baptist church strolled into the backyard, all dressed up in their Sunday finery. The choir assembled outside the thorn fence for a beautiful series of hymns. Later the church members spread out blankets and brought out hampers of barbecue and cole slaw for an old-fashioned picnic on the lawn. The tribe, however, kept a good distance between themselves and the overfriendly missionaries.

Bud also allowed two anthropologists specializing in the Maasai ethnic group and a team of *National Geographic* freelancers to document the backyard site.

When the National Cattlemen's Association and the National Milk Producers Federation came looking for free advertising on the health benefits of a diet restricted to beef and milk, and then refused to leave, Bud introduced them to Jimmy Hawk. Jimmy, who dropped by a few times a day to check on his leased cows, introduced them to his cattle prod.

Unfortunately, Bud could do nothing about the tabloid-chartered

. . . .

helicopters who sporadically buzzed the backyard village for juicy aerial shots.

The Kenyan embassy was in touch. However, the bureaucrats were too understaffed and amused to offer a solution for the Maasai tribesmen's return. On the other hand, the U.S. Immigration Service promptly offered a blanket three-month visa to the Maasai to remain, with the sole proviso that the Maasai must not accept employment during their stay. Only the warriors ventured outside the village. There were reported sightings of them strolling down the emergency lane of the Interstate, entering a Banana Republic store at an upscale mall, and creating havoc during a walk-about through a petting zoo.

Douglas and Lisa Payne could be found playing with the Maasai children from dawn until dusk. Bud and Gail both agreed that the intercultural experience was worth a few days off from school. Earlier in the day, Douglas calmly lost three straight games of mbau before he figured out his opponents' system for beating him. He won his fourth game against a much younger boy. Tepo and the other boys rewarded him with raised fists and a triumphant yell. The Maasai children, he noticed, bowed their heads to all elders. Douglas watched them carefully. They were totally for real.

Later he watched a young mother nurse her baby. Her heavy breasts were bare. Beaded necklaces fell in great loops around her neck. The baby was tremendously fat and sucked noisily, kicking its plump feet against the mother's side. Douglas tried not to embarrass the woman by watching, but she was laughing at the baby and didn't seem to mind him. In the clearing by the thorn fence, Lisa and her girlfriends stood together, singing softly, moving their hips, gently shaking dry cane stalks to their rhythm.

Of course, Fanny Butler had gone native completely. Her dress, made from calfskin imported from Argentina, was the hit of the settlement. Her mud-plastered hut, complete with bookshelves and a Coleman stove for heating water for tea, was thoroughly documented by the *National Geographic* team, who assumed her pale skin was the result of a skin disorder. With her husband in Scotland for

. . . .

the golf tournament, her comings and goings at home went even more unnoticed than usual.

Then came the moment that Fanny had been waiting for. The day before she had engaged the laibon whenever possible. For his part, the laibon avoided her troubled eyes. Finally, she sat down next to him outside his hut. She showed him a tiny toy figure of a woman, which she laid on the ground, then covered with dirt.

That night the laibon dreamed he was flying over a vast herd of cattle. He knew they were his cows. But as hard as he tried, he couldn't count them fast enough. Or remember their names. There were too many of them. He felt like weeping out of joy and frustration. When he looked down, he saw that he was wearing green scrub pants and Nike running shoes. Then, suddenly, a white person burst from the ground. Clods of dirt went flying everywhere. The white person was in flames, which he quickly put out with his hands.

When the laibon woke up, the palms of his hands were still stinging. While the morning was still very young, he stood waiting beside the cow pen. He was in luck. Reaching under the bull, the laibon rinsed off his hands and staff in the steaming piss. He remembered every detail of his dream. The person in his dream was Fanno.

From there the laibon walked to Fanny's hut. Inside, she was shaving her scalp with a safety razor. She saw the laibon in her hand mirror nod gravely, then beckon her outside.

A few minutes later, Fanny began digging a long, narrow hole in the clearing outside the thorn fence.

. . . .

TWENTY-ONE

"Don't worry about dinner, Gail. We'll grab something after the movie," Lilly said. Douglas and Lisa followed her to the back door."

"Douglas and Lisa, be good," Gail called out, waving goodbye.

"Mom?" said Lisa. She hesitated at the door. "Fanny told me and Douglas a secret."

Douglas gave his little sister a warning glance. "Lisa!"

"It's not a good secret if someone can get hurt by it, right, Mom?"

Gail's maternal radar was up as she knelt in front of Lisa. "That's right, Lisa. What did Fanny tell you?"

"She said the laibon is going to fix her basket case today."

"What?"

"Wrong." Douglas shook his head. "Fanny said *she's* a basket case. But the laibon can fix that."

"How?"

"Mom, the laibon buried Fanny alive in our backyard." The words rushed out of Lisa like air escaping from a balloon.

"Nice going, Lisa," said her brother.

From the kitchen window, Gail saw the laibon, elders, and families standing over a fresh mound of dirt—Fanny's grave. She shut her eyes for a second, then picked up the phone.

"Let's go, kids," said Lilly, yanking them out the door. "We don't want to miss the coming attractions."

"I need an ambulance," Gail told Bud's service. "And tell Bud to come home immediately."

Bertram Butler dropped his suitcase and golf bag in the foyer of his house. "Peewee?" he called. "Peewee?" He listened carefully. No pitter-patter of little pig feet across the wood floors. Just the steady tick-tock of the grandfather clock.

He glanced in the mirror, and straightened the pompom on his souvenir hat. All the golfers at the Scottish Invitational had received one. Why did bright clothes and funny hats seem to go with the game of golf, he wondered.

"Peewee?" He heard a dripping faucet in the kitchen. "Fanny?"

Bertram opened the kitchen door and stepped out on his raised wooden deck. All was quiet in his backyard. But there was some sort of a commotion over in the Paynes'. Mud-plastered huts. Cows. Thorn fence. African elders, tall and slender, dressed in blankets, standing over a fresh mound of dirt. Gail Payne, agitated, shouting, sprinting toward them.

"What in the world is going on?" Bertram muttered.

Bud never slowed down as he turned the corner of the garage. Gail was pleading with the laibon near the mound. An ambulance wailed in the background. Bertram Butler, wearing yellow slacks and green blazer, was striding toward them with a four iron. The pompom on his hat bounced up and down like a child's paddleball game.

"Bud, do something!" said Gail, pointing at the mound. "She's down there."

"Who's down there?" Bertram asked.

"Fanny."

"Let me explain," Bud said.

"Fanny?" Bertram said, obviously disoriented. "Where's Peewee?"

"Fanny and Peewee are okay." Bud stepped between Gail and Bertram. "I've seen the Maasai laibon perform this same procedure in Kenya. All it involves is oxygen deprivation and—"

"What procedure, Dr. Payne?" Bertram's face was flushed.

. . . .

117

"Primitive shock therapy, that's all it is."

"What is?"

"Bud, do something!" cried Gail. "Fanny and Peewee are buried alive."

"Wait a minute. Are you trying to tell me that Fanny and Peewee are buried alive down there?" Bertram cried out.

"Yes," Bud and Gail replied at the same time.

Bertram sat down heavily on the ground. "I don't feel so good."

Three EMTs jogged toward them carrying large medical bags, oxygen, and a stretcher.

"Where is she?" asked the first EMT.

"Down there," said Gail. "Hurry."

"Wait a minute! Stop!" said Bud. "I'm Dr. Payne. This is my backyard. The woman buried here consented to a procedure that I've seen this healer perform in Kenya. Believe me, this man has got everything under control."

The EMTs stared at the haughty laibon, Bertram on the ground, the shallow grave, then Bud. The first EMT spoke for all of them. "I don't think so. Let's get her out."

The rescue team knelt down and began furiously scooping the loose dirt out with their hands.

The laibon understood that Payne had tried to defend his methods. These men, dressed in blue, were from another tribe. Perhaps they were Fanno's brothers and were acting under the orders of their tribal healer. Gathering his robes around him, he returned to the settlement.

"I've got her," said the youngest EMT, his arm buried up to his elbow in the dirt. Carefully, he and his partner lifted Fanny out of the hole, laying her on the stretcher.

Gail covered his mouth with her hand. "Oh, Fanny. What have you done?"

The senior EMT unknotted the canvas sack around Fanny's shoulders and slid it off her head. He blew the dust off her face.

"She's got a pulse. But it's weak."

"We've got to get her to Hiassen Memorial Hospital. Stat."

Gail glanced down at Bertram, who seemed immobile, even at the

· · · ·

mention of taking his wife to a competing hospital. "I'll go with her," said Gail. She stayed alongside the stretcher as the EMTs hustled back to the ambulance.

Suddenly a loud squealing was heard from the hole. Bertram eyes opened wide. "Peewee!"

The little pig nosed his head out, squirmed out of the half-buried sack, then scrambled out of the hole.

"Bertram, let me explain," said Bud.

"No explanation is necessary, Dr. Payne." Bertram scrambled to his feet. "Not only have you endangered my wife and pig, you've violated every moral code of your profession."

Bertram scooped Peewee up in his arms. "As chairperson of the board of Tully Hospital, I am suspending your privileges as of now. Later, when things have calmed down, I'll see that your license is permanently revoked."

"Now, if you'll excuse me," said Bertram. "I'd like to take Peewee to the vet for a brain scan."

TWENTY-TWO

Bud stared into the computer screen. He couldn't remember the house ever being this quiet during the middle of the day. In fact, he couldn't remember ever being home in the middle of the day. He started typing rapidly. He wasn't sure if he was doing the right thing, but it felt good. The ghosts began chasing the goblins across the graveyard in Douglas's computer game.

On the tenth chime, Bud realized the sound was coming from the front door, not the computer.

He was greeted by a woman's smile. A famous smile that enchanted millions of television viewers every week. Although he didn't have time for afternoon talk shows, Bud knew the woman better than he knew his neighbor across the street.

"Oprah Winfrey?"

"Dr. Payne?"

Behind Oprah's smile, a large crew of GNN production assistants and technicians gathered on his front steps. "Yes?" He swallowed heavily as he shook her diamond-braceleted hand.

"It's a pleasure to meet you. I heard about your story when it first broke. And since I was in town giving a commencement address, I thought I'd stop by and catch you at home. Can I come in?"

"I don't know . . ." Bud wasn't sure what to do with the hand she was still holding. "The house is a real mess."

"Oh, goody. I'll feel right at home."

Ninety minutes later, Oprah leaned forward on the couch next to Bud. Her legs crossed, her arm draped over the back of the couch, she made Bud feel like a stranger on his own sofa.

"So how did Gail react to the news that thirty Maasai warriors, elders, women, and children would be sharing your home?"

"She was very supportive." Bud didn't know why, but it seemed the most natural thing to say to a talk show host.

The GNN cameras were rolling. Oprah's producer and technicians crowded into the living room filled with lights and power cords.

"But later, when they destroyed her meticulously landscaped backyard to erect their mud huts and thorn fence—were there many tears?"

"Yes, of course. It was quite a shock."

"I'll say." Oprah smiled straight at the camera. "It's a fascinating story, Dr. Payne. Later we'll be going to the hospital to meet with the young child and her mother. But first, one last question. Bud, I have to ask you this. The entire tribe flew over at your expense, right?"

"That's correct."

"Do you feel . . . taken advantage of?"

"Well . . ."

"Your backyard is devastated." Oprah counted on her fingertips. "You owe thousands of dollars to a local dairy farmer. Your neighbor was buried alive. And you may lose the right to practice medicine. Do you feel like someone owes you an explanation?"

"Well, everything has happened so fast, you understand . . ."

"Which member of the tribe spoke up and allowed you to bring Hope and her family members over here?"

"That would be Kimo."

"If my neighbor was buried alive, and my career was shot down, I would certainly want Kimo to answer some questions."

"Why are you doing this to me?" Bud demanded, gripping his cordless phone.

. . . .

Kimo, relaxing in the shade of his hut, glanced up. His expression didn't change.

"Why does a tribe of seminomadic herdsmen and -women suddenly pull up stakes, leave everything behind, to fly to the U.S. and screw me to the wall?"

A look of annoyance flickered across Kimo's face.

"I want answers." Bud spoke into the phone. "Go ahead, Cynthia. Ask him."

Getting to his feet, Kimo entered his hut without a word.

"Don't just walk away, Kimo. I want an answer. I'm not leaving until you tell me why you came."

Bud stood there and glared at the hut opening. "I need to know! So does my wife, American Express, and Oprah Winfrey!"

Warriors, elders, the laibon, and others drifted closer to Kimo's hut to check out the normally quiet doctor.

"Talk to me! Man to man! But don't tell me you came because of Hope. Because I know it's something more than that. Why did you bring the whole village to my backyard?"

More silence from the hut.

"Dammit, Kimo! I've put up with a lot from you! I'm not taking any more. That's it!"

Bud kicked the side of Kimo's hut. Hard. Unexpectedly, his foot punched through the mud plaster and snagged on the interlaced branches. When Bud tried to yank his leg free, the hut trembled. He tugged harder. The wall collapsed into a heap of limbs and dried clay.

Bud tripped, falling heavily onto his back. The phone landed a few feet away. Before he could get to his feet, Kimo rushed out. His eyes were flaming hot. He grabbed a long spear out of a warrior's hand and lowered the razor-sharp steel blade against Bud's chest.

"What are you doing?" cried Bud.

Kimo's face was hard, cold, and sweaty. "You violated my house. Even your law says I can kill you for that."

Bud felt the tip of the blade prick his chest. "You speak English. I wasn't dreaming."

"Yes. You want to hear more?"

. . . .

122

Bud gritted his teeth. "Yes."

"You demand to know why we came to your backyard. But did we ask why you came to our backyard in Kenya?"

"No."

"What's the difference?"

"I came to help you."

"You came to give away your knowledge and technology," Kimo said harshly.

"What's wrong with that?"

"What did you ask in return?"

"Nothing."

Kimo moved the spear up—pointing the tip under Bud's chin. "Nothing. Why is that?"

Bud was silent.

"You asked for nothing because you believe you have all the answers. Because you believe we have nothing to give. But there is one thing you take from us each time you come. The most important thing—our pride."

Kimo suddenly flipped the spear back to the warrior. His eyes were still bright, but the fires had cooled. "I wanted my people to come here so they could see what your world is like. Now they know that you don't have all the answers. They look around. They see how you subdivide your land, your hearts, your heads, and call it progress. You value time over everything, but you don't have time for anything."

Bud slowly got to his feet. "Why did you wait to tell me this?"

"Because you don't listen."

"And you do? You're not perfect either. You're locked in the past. You believe it's bad luck to look ahead. The Maasai could operate the world's greatest cattle farms, but that would take planning and education. You'd have to stop hiding behind your spears and shields. And start educating your children—even the girls."

One of the Maasai women pushed her way to the front of the warriors. In halting English she said, "Kimo speaks for only himself. Myself and the others, we came here to be with our little Opana. That's all."

. . . .

Bud and Kimo continued to stare at each other. For a moment, no one dared move. Then, out of the corner of his eye, Bud saw Chandler approach.

"Nice day," Chandler said casually.

"What are you doing here?" asked Bud.

"I was in the neighborhood when a candystriper called me on another line." He picked up Bud's cordless phone from the ground and spoke into it, "See you soon, Cynthia."

"Oh," said Bud. So Cynthia had heard the argument and notified Chandler.

"We've scheduled Hope's heart surgery for this afternoon. It might be nice if you and the laibon came by to see her first."

TWENTY-THREE

WORLD PREMIERE MOVIE TONIGHT: High Plains Slasher, *Part 1,* read the marquee sign posted in front of the Maasai global village. Zach scanned the list of credits. Written and directed by Loomo. Executive producer: Zach Tyler.

Zach found Loomo in the editing hut adding the final touches to his slasher film. The room hummed with the whirring of the audio track and whizzing of tape and gears. Loomo kept one eye on the monitor as his hands fluttered over dials and buttons, backing up, erasing.

In the corner, a few children were sitting in front of the GNN News monitor. Zach had resorted to super-gluing the channel selector to GNN. The elders grumbled and stayed away now that they could no longer watch "World Championship Wrestling."

"Loomo, I noticed your film says Part One. I thought we agreed on no more slasher films?" This was still a delicate subject. Zach believed the global village should produce videos that revealed mankind's universal themes and hopes. Loomo, on the other hand, believed they should produce videos that were commercial and scared people witless.

"Well, Zach," Loomo finally said, hunched over at the tiny playback monitor. "Marketing thought the 'One' would be a strong selling point."

"Who is Marketing?" Zach asked.

"I am."

"I see. So the Part One is a little misleading."

"No. If I said it was Part Two, that would be misleading. But it is Part One."

"But doesn't that imply there's going to be Part Two?"

"If I have one birthday, does that imply I'm going to have two?" Loomo kept his eyes focused on the tape counter. "No, of course not. I could be eaten by a lion, bitten by a mamba, or anything."

On the monitor, a GNN reporter was standing in front of a long soup line in some cold, gray city (Detroit? Belgrade?). Zach was beginning to suspect that he and Loomo would never find a middle ground of agreement.

"Are you bringing Liz to the world premiere?" Loomo asked.

Zach made a face. Ever since he'd met the adventurous flying doctor, Loomo had assumed the worst—or best. Zach hadn't decided yet.

"I don't think so. Liz says that any culture that glorifies raping, maiming, torturing, or slashing young women over making love to them is sick."

He neglected to mention that Liz had also said that giving the warriors videocams was like putting a loaded gun in their hands and telling them not to use it except for self-defense.

Someone knocked on the door of the Quonset hut. "Anyone home?"

"Come in," Loomo called out.

"Are you expecting someone?" asked Zach.

"GNN."

"The Global News Network?" Zach asked excitedly. GNN was the key to the global village. His letters and prayers had finally been answered.

The GNN crew piled into the Quonset hut with appreciative oohs and aahs at the state-of-the-art editing board.

Loomo spread out his arms. "Welcome to the world premiere of *High Plains Slasher, Part One.*"

. . . .

TWENTY-FOUR

"C'mon, let's go." Chandler, dressed in green surgeon scrubs, stood in the doorway of the doctors' locker room.

"Just a minute." Bud walked behind the laibon, who wore green scrubs just like Chandler's. Except for the long earlobes that dangled out of the laibon's tight-fitting green cap, he looked like your typical resident surgeon.

Moments later, the three doctors walked past the nurses' station. The head nurse nodded absentmindedly at them, then noticed a pair of long, rubber-band-like earlobes. She picked up the phone. "Someone needs to notify the administrator that the witch doctor is back."

In the chief administrator's office, Richard Moorehead sat behind his desk, working two calls at the same time.

"Hello, sir," said the voice over the intercom. "Are you there?"

"Yes? What did you find out?" asked Richard. He had been referred to the New Orleans Voodoo Shoppe by Sister Alicia, a palm reader on Highway 129.

"Sounds like your man used a rhino-horn baton to deliver that below-the-belt punch."

"What do you advise my friend to do?"

"Let me check. Hold on."

Richard punched the other line. "Sorry to keep you waiting, Dr. Gravelines."

. . . .

"No problem, Mr. Moorehead," the urologist replied without enthusiasm. "Is there some problem with the Medicaid reimbursement forms?"

"No, those are fine. Actually, I have a friend who wanted me to ask you a delicate question."

"A friend?" Dr. Gravelines asked skeptically.

"Yes, but not a close friend. Just someone I met recently. A fellow skydiver. He says his thing is shrinking."

"His thing?"

"Can you hold?" Richard pushed the other line. "Well?" he asked the voodoo clerk.

"That's a real heavy-duty curse, Mr. Smith. Your friend must've done something totally atrocious."

"I didn't do anything! Can you help me? Him?"

"I can order it. Takes three months."

Richard slammed the phone button. "So, Dr. Gravelines? Is there anything in the literature about that?"

"You mean the shrinking thing literature?"

"Oh, they have a special category for it?"

"Of course, Mr. Moorehead."

"Then what can I do?" he sputtered. "He do? About voodoo?"

"There's only one cure."

Richard sat forward on the edge of his chair. "Yes?"

"Tell your friend to get a good magnifying glass."

Richard was still pondering his next move when his receptionist opened the door and poked her head in. "Mr. Moorehead, the witch doctor is headed toward Hope's room with Dr. Payne."

Hope held out her arms to greet Bud. Then she eyed the tall, suited-up surgeon next to him. A big smile spread across her face as she reached up to hug the laibon.

"There he is! Arrest the witch doctor." Richard ran into the room, pointing out the laibon to three young security guards. In his effort to keep directly out of the line of fire, however, Richard tripped over a power cord. Alarms from Hope's monitors rang out.

· · · ·

The laibon's first reaction was to save the child. He quickly lifted Hope in his arms, cradling her to his chest.

"What are you doing?" said a young nurse. "Watch out for her IVs!"

As the monitor alarms rang, the nurses reacted quickly to prevent the IVs from pulling out. Alarms were going off at the nurses station: *"Code Blue!" "Code Blue!"*

"What is he doing?" Chandler asked calmly.

Cynthia told the laibon in Swahili, "Put her down!"

"No. I'm taking her home," the laibon replied.

"Not now," Cynthia said. "It's time for surgery."

"Enough has passed. Once I stopped you from breaking her heart. Twice your warriors have stopped me from healing your sick. Now the evil red-haired one has returned. Why should I trust you?"

Bud asked, "What did he say?"

Cynthia told them, then added, "Breaking that plastic heart was a bad omen. He wants to take her back to Kenya. Without surgery."

"She won't make it," Chandler said anxiously.

"That's the final straw," said Richard. "Hostage-taking will not be tolerated at Tully Hospital." He pointed at the laibon, then thought better of it, stepped back, and stood behind a security guard. "Put the child down. I'll count to three."

"Wait a minute," Bud turned to Cynthia. "Tell the laibon it's not his decision to make."

"I think he's already decided, Dr. Payne."

"One . . ." Richard counted.

"Then tell him I'll bring the oloiboni here to decide. He'll listen to him!" Bud exclaimed.

While Cynthia translated, Bud explained to Chandler that the oloiboni was a Maasai mystic in Kenya who spoke directly to God.

"Just what we need," said an exasperated Chandler. "Another specialist."

"Two . . ." said Richard.

The laibon's eyes widened with interest.

"But it'll take days to fly him here," Cynthia said to Bud.

"No, we can do better than that."

· · · ·

"Three . . ."

Before Richard could give the final order, Oprah Winfrey burst through the door with her staff right behind her.

"Oprah!" cried out Richard. "What are you doing here?"

"We have a few fans inside the hospital." Oprah winked at Bud. "The head nurse tipped us off."

Bud quickly explained the situation to Oprah. He told her about the oloiboni and all about Zach Tyler and his high-tech communications equipment. If Oprah could linkup with Zach . . .

Oprah's producer waved her portable phone and got her star's attention. "You won't believe this, but we've got a reporter covering a world premiere movie in a Maasai settlement. We'll see if we can get some satellite time. It's worth a try."

Ten minutes later, Oprah raised her fist excitedly. "We've got Zach and the satellite. Everything's go."

The TV monitor over Hope's bed flashed on. "We interrupt our regularly scheduled programming to bring you this special report."

Oprah began talking into the camera, then appeared on the TV monitor after a one-second delay. The laibon did a double-take.

"Good afternoon. This is Oprah Winfrey. Thank you for allowing me into your home on this very dramatic occasion. And thank GNN for making this possible."

Around the world, hundreds of millions of people stopped what they were doing to watch the drama unfold.

Douglas and Lisa sprawled out on the floor of Lilly's town house and watched their father in the same room as Oprah on the large Zenith console.

Niu-phon Linh, the Korean woman who had been healed by the laibon, called her family together at the Lucky Star Restaurant. She pointed excitedly at the laibon on TV, then at her healed arm.

At the Kilbezi Clinic in Kenya, Sister Beth joined the other nuns in front of the clinic TV.

Meanwhile, at Hiaasen Memorial Hospital, Fanny was resting quietly. In the grave, she had felt an overwhelming peacefulness. Her thoughts, usually rumbling and tumbling together like an afternoon storm, had become so calm she felt she was on a heavenly

· · · ·

vacation. The weight of the dirt on her head, chest, and legs had been more soothing than she could have ever imagined. Being buried alive wasn't so bad. Years of scuba diving and spelunking had prepared her for the worst. Yet the whole time she was buried in the womb of the earth, she had felt the laibon's thoughts and prayers lapping through her.

Suddenly, she sat up in bed and pointed Oprah out to Gail.

Oprah was saying, "For those of you following the story, it's become a tense standoff between the wishes of the tribal healer and the official policies of a modern hospital."

"We've got to help Bud," said Gail. She felt a new surge of love and protectiveness for her husband. Once again Bud was trying to walk a fine line of respect between both cultures. He had tried it with Fanny and the laibon, but was no match for the EMTs and Bertram. Now he was trying again. And this time Gail would be there to back him up.

Fanny threw off the covers and bounded out of bed in her hospital gown. "I'm right behind you, Gail. But we need wheels."

The young woman in the bed next to them held up her car keys. "Hey, girls! You can borrow my car if you bring me back a cheese-burger and shake."

On TV, Oprah chose her words carefully. "Every day more and more tragedies are played out in front of television cameras. Well, today, we hope to avert one. At the center of our hopes and dreams is one child." The camera zoomed in for a closeup of Hope lying in the laibon's arms.

"Heel to toe. Heel to toe," Gail mumbled to herself, as she down-shifted the TransAm past three cows, then spun out in the dirt clearing in her own backyard. Leaning out the window, Fanny checked out the shallow hole she'd been laid to rest in earlier.

Gail laid on the horn. Warriors, elders, women, and children came running. "Bud and the laibon need reinforcements at the hospital."

Without hesitating, Kimo nodded at the warriors. They hoisted their spears, moving toward the car.

. . . .

131

"Not you," said Gail, pointing. "Them."

Kimo turned around and stared at the beaming faces of the Maasai women. They shouldered their way past the warriors. In halting English, one of the women turned to Gail. "We are ready."

"Road trip!" Fanny called out.

Gail floored it and the muscle car fishtailed, spinning out in the dirt. They passed the three-car garage, bounced over the curb, and roared down the street. The goat woman stared out the rear window at the distant sight of Kimo and the warriors, carrying spears and shields, running down the center lane behind them.

"Now we'd like to take you to Kenya for a live satellite hookup in the plains far below Mount Kilimanjaro," said Oprah. She gazed up at the TV monitor over the bed.

Static . . . hissing . . . electronic bleeting . . . then . . .

"Yes, Oprah, we're here in Kenya, about three hours from Nairobi, outside the Amboseli Game Reserve. That's Mount Kilimanjaro you see in the background."

The GNN reporter, dressed in khakis, walked up a steep, rocky incline while talking into his microphone.

"Wow," said Bud. Even he had trouble believing this was actually happening. He rubbed his eyes. Walking beside the GNN reporter in Kenya was ex-kiddy show host, ex-aislemate Zach Tyler.

"Edward, have you made contact with the spiritual leader of the Maasai people?"

"Oprah, I'm being taken there right now by an American, Zach Tyler, who resides in a nearby village. The oloiboni lives on a narrow outcropping of rock here. It's not much farther."

"Edward, I'm sure our viewers would be interested in hearing how we are able to cover both sides of the Atlantic on this ongoing story."

"Well, it may seem unbelievable, but . . ."

The screen went blank.

"Out of Africa! Get me out of Africa!" the GNN cameraman screamed on the ground. His ankle was bent at a funny angle from

· · · ·

his leg. His body was sore and bruised from rolling down the steep incline while trying to protect the camera.

Edward flipped the microphone against his pressed khakis. Seconds were ticking off. The world was waiting for his broadcast.

"Shake it off!" Edward shouted to the cameraman. "C'mon, get up! We're live!"

"Owww!"

"It's a torn tendon." Zach Tyler knelt beside the fallen cameraman.

"But we've got a story to do!"

Zach asked several of the young Maasai warriors to pick up the moaning cameraman and carry him back to the village. One of the warriors lifted the camera off the ground. He held it up in the air and examined it closely.

Edward frowned. "Be careful with that. That's an extremely expensive piece of equipment."

Zach watched Mbwo. "He's never seen a professional betacam before," he told Edward.

As Edward watched helplessly, Mbwo turned the camera around in his hands while he and Zach carried on an animated conversation. Finally Zach turned back to Edward. "You see, Mbwo has never shot one-inch video. I told him it's the same as half-inch."

Mbwo shouldered the camera, then expertly framed the GNN announcer in a tight shot.

"What are we waiting for?" Edward called out excitedly. "Looks like I've got a new cameraman!"

Now the laibon understood why the whites were always watching the boxes. He finally saw something that made sense. Inside the box over Opana's bed was the oloiboni. In the distance was the cone-shaped peak of Kilimanjaro rising into the clouds. He hugged Opana to his chest.

"Oprah, can you hear me?" The GNN reporter in Kenya was standing in front of a small hut that stood alone on a small outcropping of rock. Behind him stood Zach and a few Maasai elders.

"Yes," Oprah replied.

. . . .

The screen split in half. Oprah and the hospital room drama on one side, Edward and the oloiboni on the other.

The laibon walked in front of Oprah, facing the camera. "Father, do you see me?"

There was a slight delay.

"Yes." The holy man nodded with his upper body. "You are never out of my sight."

"Then you know my question," said the laibon. "How does God answer it?"

"I will ask." The oloiboni knelt down, taking out his polished cow horn. He poured the smooth stones on the ground, then studied their arrangement. He picked the pebbles up one by one, then scattered them again.

The laibon and others watched TV anxiously.

"He's making a laughing stock out of us." Richard fidgeted. "I won't tolerate any more voodoo in this hospital." He turned to the three security guards.

"Secure the child."

Before they could move, Gail, Fanny, and the Maasai women crowded into the room between the laibon and the guards. The women locked arms.

Gail said, "You'll have to get through us first." She smiled at Bud. "How are we doing?"

"Great," he said. But a quick glance at Hope immediately proved him wrong. He reached the laibon's side, listening carefully to her breathing, squeezing out every other sound in the room.

"Jerome, come here," Bud said.

The heart monitor alarm began beeping.

Hope gasped for air. The laibon continued to hold her, but his eyes were troubled.

"Florid congestive heart failure," said Chandler, pressing his ear against the child's chest. "We've got to move fast."

On TV, the oloiboni reached out and picked up the pebbles lying on the ground one by one.

Chandler held out his arms in front of the laibon. "You need to trust me."

· · · ·

The Maasai women turned around to face their healer. Pika, who had been quiet until now, pleaded gently with him. But the laibon's eyes were fixed on the screen.

Then, Cynthia translated the oloiboni's words: "He says that God let us choose so that we can love God more. As for the child, he says we should choose what is best in her interest, not ours."

Edward smiled into the camera. "We hope that's the news you've been waiting for, Oprah."

"Yes, it is," said Oprah, holding the microphone aloft as everyone in the room cheered.

In front of the TV in Lilly's town house, Lisa's eyes were wet. "Hope's going to be okay, isn't she?"

"Isn't it wonderful to think of a hundred million people from Peking to Peoria viewing a sweet story like that?" Sister Claire sighed. "Children are mankind's greatest blessing."

"All that fuss over one child," Sister Lucille muttered as she turned off the TV. "With all that time and money, we could distribute penicillin and save thousands of children from disease."

"When a ship sinks, you save anyone you can," said Liz. "You don't stop to design a safer vessel."

"What if two hundred people drown while you're saving one?" argued Sister Lucille.

"What if you're the one, Sister?" said Liz.

Zach burst into Loomo's hut. "Did you catch GNN?" he asked out of breath.

"You were great!" Loomo said. He got off his bench and shook Zach's hand. "I couldn't believe it."

"I told you, Loomo. Didn't I tell you? This is the age of the televillage. It doesn't matter where you live. Minneapolis or Maasailand. We're all neighbors. We're all links on the same chain!" Zach pounded his fist. "And, by God, it's time we started pulling together!"

"Zach, I'm pulling the plug on *High Plains Slasher*."

. . . .

"But why? You worked so hard on it."

"During editing, I took out everything that didn't make sense. At the end, I only had one minute left."

"A Maasai Minute," said Zach, excitedly. "I can't wait to see it."

TWENTY-FIVE

Suddenly Gail sat up in bed. The room was dark and quiet, except for Bud's breathing. Then she heard it again. It was just outside their bedroom door. She tapped Bud's shoulder.

"There's someone in the house."

Bud snapped awake. He held his breath, then a few seconds later, he heard it. Down the hallway they tiptoed in their pajamas. Gail thought it was strange, but Douglas and Lisa were standing in their doorways. Douglas gripped his trusty Louisville Slugger.

"What is it?" Lisa whispered.

Now, in single file behind Bud, they entered the kitchen.

"It's outside on the deck," said Gail.

They stood against the customized cabinets, behind the kitchen island, when . . .

The window above the kitchen sink exploded as the full-grown lion hurtled through. The Paynes covered their eyes as the glass shattered across the room.

The beast slid across the linoleum, his talons scratching and clattering, then stopped ten feet away from them, arched his back, then froze them with his gleaming eyes. His mouth opened wide, revealing rows of yellowish fangs, and a hiss like escaping gas.

They were too shocked to speak, or move. Except for Bud. Slowly he raised the beeper that was gripped tightly in his hand.

. . . .

The lion crouched lower, ready to spring.

Then, somehow, Kimo materialized in front of them. His face was calm, expressionless, as he stretched his arm toward the lion, then stepped forward. The lion crept toward the hand, then sniffed it carefully, before giving it a big, sloppy lick.

Startled awake, Gail opened her eyes. Across the waiting room the Maasai tribe had gathered near the wide window facing the hospital grounds.

"I dreamed that we were about to be attacked by a lion," she told Bud.

"What happened?"

"Kimo saved us." She straightened up. "I've been thinking about what Kimo said to you. At first I thought he was very ungrateful. But now I think he was right about some things. We gave them the best gift we have—our medical know-how. But maybe he's been giving us the best gift they have."

"What's that?"

"I think they came to teach us a lesson. To show us how they could live in harmony anywhere—even in our backyard. And I think he's too proud to tell us that was his gift."

Lilly was walking toward them with Douglas and Lisa.

"Dad, we saw you on TV," Lisa called out.

"You were cool," said Douglas.

Less than an hour later, the doors marked AUTHORIZED PERSONNEL swung open. Dr. Chandler and Cynthia Goodman slowly approached the hushed waiting room. Chandler walked past Bud, then stopped in front of the laibon. He said in Swahili, while Cynthia beamed at her proud student, "She's fine. The operation was a great success."

The laibon raised his clenched fist triumphantly in the air. The others began enthusiastically hugging each other.

"We replaced the mitral valve," Chandler turned around and said to Bud. "No complications. I'll give it my unconditional one-million-mile or one-hundred-year guarantee, whichever comes first."

"We need to celebrate," said Bud, embracing Gail and the chil-

· · · ·

dren. Across the room he saw Kimo smile. "Harambee?" Bud called out.

Kimo studied him for a few moments, then replied, "Harambee."

Everyone in the waiting room picked up the refrain. "Harambee, harambee, harambee . . ."

TWENTY-SIX

Gail poured tea and served cake to the Maasai women sitting at the kitchen table. It was the day following Hope's surgery and the women were clearly at ease, talking and laughing. Speeding to the hospital, linking arms in front of the security guards, had bonded them in a way they'd never forget—or let the warriors live down.

As Mamta, who spoke halting English, explained, "We are proud of you and ourselves."

Mamta translated a woman's question. "She says you look happy now. Are you pregnant?"

"I hope not," said Gail. "We're happy with two children. We're not planning on having any more."

Mamta broke the news. The Maasai women shook their heads sympathetically. "Without many children we wouldn't be happy. Our men wouldn't be happy."

Another Maasai woman added, "Children take care of us when we're old and without teeth."

Gail wondered if it was worth going into a lecture on birth control. Instead, she asked if the women missed Kenya.

"Yes," said Mamta, adding, "but in Kenya we work all day to bring water, find wood, cook, and take care of the children and cows and goats. We did not have so much work to do in your backyard."

"But what do the men do all day?" Gail asked.

Mamta translated amid much shouting and laughing. "They are too busy being men to do much else. Women do all the work."

"In my grandmother's day," said Gail, "it was like that for women here. But then roads were built, electricity brought lights and appliances, and pipes brought water. Girls began receiving the same education as boys. Men and women began to share more work. Also, women began to stick together and help each other."

After relaying Gail's words to the women, Mamta said, "Perhaps things will begin to change for us. Perhaps our granddaughters will be like you."

"Not like me," Gail said. "I hope our granddaughters take the best from you and me." Then Gail added, "And I hope that our grandsons help them."

Later, Gail led the women on a room-by-room tour of the house. As she opened up yet another room to their awestruck eyes, she began to feel more and more embarrassed. Why had the Paynes accumulated so much? She tried to reassure herself by saying her stockpile was light compared to those of her more materialistic friends. But, nonetheless, in front of these proud, simple women, Gail felt positively decadent.

The bonfire licked at the sky, then sent up a fine dancing spray of sparks to mingle in the heavens.

Surrounding the bonfire, filling the backyard as far as the eye could see, people were celebrating at the Paynes' backyard harambee.

Bud shouldered his way through the surging crowd. He thanked Dean Martin for handling security, and congratulated Jimmy Hawk on how happy his remaining cows looked. He exchanged words with fellow doctors, nurses, orderlies, patients, gospel singers, skateboarders, off-duty journalists, cameramen—everyone who had been touched in some way by the visiting tribe.

A gospel choir was singing beside the fig tree. In another corner of the backyard, the sounds of Dixieland jazz reverberated across the

. . . .

huts where Maasai warriors aimed their bodies high in the air, performing their bottle-rocket-like dance.

Cynthia Goodman stood behind Hope, who was seated in a wheelchair, dressed in her beaded finery.

A long line of people danced in a conga line up to a sisal basket, manned by Dr. Chandler and his fiancée, Gloria, who were encouraging everyone to donate funds to reimburse the Paynes' expenses. The sounds of singing, laughter, and children's voices filled the air as Richard Moorehead sidled through the crowd. He entered the thorn fence, and stepped around another line of people queued in front of a hut. At that moment, an elderly woman stepped out of the hut. She flexed both of her hands with gusto. "I haven't been able to do this in years," she explained. "The stiffness is completely gone!"

The laibon poked his head out. He saw the administrator get down on his knees.

"Hey, get to the end of the line," someone called out.

Richard murmured, "This is an emergency."

The laibon hesitated, then motioned him inside.

On the other side of the backyard village, Bud, Gail, Douglas, and Lisa approached Kimo, who watched the celebration from a distance.

"I owe you an apology," said Bud, watching Kimo's expressionless face. "I had no right to kick in your hut."

"And my family and I want to thank you for coming," said Gail. "I think we've all learned something from your being here."

"Thank you," said Kimo.

"How'd you learn to speak English?" asked Lisa.

"Like I told your father, I drove a cab out of Heathrow Airport in London for three years. I was in law school at the time."

"Wow!" exclaimed Douglas. "A Maasai lawyer!"

"So what's next?" Bud asked.

As if in reply, Kimo picked up a spear leaning against the hut, hefted it in his hand, then took two steps and hurled it away. *Thwack!* The spear hit the bull's-eye—a tall pole standing upright in the bonfire.

. . . .

"Change is hard on everyone, but especially for us. If we return to live by our old ways, we become a tourist attraction. If we change too much, we lose ourselves," he said with a gentle smile. "Life is hard, but the Maasai believe that a hard life with meaning is better than an easy life without meaning." He held his hand out toward Bud. "What I said to you before wasn't fair. I was angry. I thank you for your friendship and respect. I'm proud of our honorary family."

The line outside the laibon's hut stretched around the huts and out the entrance to the thorn fence by the time Richard finally emerged. There was a sarcastic smattering of applause. Richard grinned proudly at the crowd. He rolled, cocked, and gyrated his hips, then broke into "I feel goooood . . ." with a James Brown howl.

In another corner of the backyard, Gail stopped by the makeshift bar to see how the drinks were holding up. She was leaning over the cooler when she heard a high-pitched voice that sent shivers down her back.

"Oh, Mrs. Payne. I've been looking everywhere for you," said Mrs. Laplace, editor-in-chief of *Backyard Magazine.*

"I'm so sorry," Gail said. "I've been meaning to apologize . . ."

"No, no, no. I owe you an apology. I should've called sooner. We need you to okay this press proof for our next cover. What do you think?"

The magazine cover took Gail's breath away. Below the magazine's familiar masthead was a stunning four-color photo of the sun setting over Gail's backyard with the thorn fence and mud-plastered huts. It was entitled in big bold letters THE NEW BACKYARD.

"I don't know what to say," said Gail.

"We think it reveals a different aesthetic—one of the heart."

Bud walked up behind Gail and studied the cover as she initialized it. "Congratulations, dear."

"Thank you, Mrs. Payne," said Mrs. Laplace, as she left with the proof.

Bud embraced Gail. "How does it feel to be a pioneer in backyard village landscaping?"

Before she could reply, Fanny and Bertram approached them,

. . . .

walking arm in arm. Peewee trailed behind them with another potbellied pig.

"Great party, Paynes," said Bertram.

"Bertram? Fanno?" Bud said in complete astonishment. He couldn't remember the last time he had seen them this close together.

Fanny corrected him, "It's Fanny."

Bud and Gail stared at a big purplish mark on Bertram's neck.

"What are you staring at?" asked Bertram. "Haven't you ever seen a hickey before?"

"Ever since they dug her out, she's been a hellcat." He squeezed her waist. "You know the first thing she did when she came home? Threw my golf bags out the second-story window."

"He said I should've done it ten years ago," Fanny cut in.

"Hell, yes. I didn't realize how much I hated the game until those clubs went out the window. Do you have any idea how hard it is to hit that tiny ball into a little bitty hole?"

Fanny nudged her husband. "Tell him the news."

"Oh, yes. I dropped that silly little ethics thing at the hospital. You can go back to work tomorrow."

Bud and Gail glanced at each other.

"I don't think so," Bud said.

"Why not?"

"We've decided that we need some time off."

"But what are you going to do?" asked Fanny.

"Time will tell," answered Gail.

The black-topped highway shimmered beneath the bright afternoon sun, cutting a black groove through rural Alabama countryside. The dusty rental car followed the winding highway, then turned onto a dirt road.

An old, wood-framed house stood at the end of the dirt road. Insects buzzed from the fields and woods that stretched out on all sides of the house.

On the front porch, a lazy hound dog lifted its head next to the rocking chair, opened one eye in the direction of the car, then slapped its head back down again.

From inside the house came the sound of running footsteps. Then the front screen door flew open. Douglas and Lisa, in their early twenties, stood in the doorway.

"She's here!" said Douglas.

"They're here, Dad!"

Bud came through the door behind them. The full, grayish beard made him look even older than he was, but the Braves baseball cap he wore betrayed a youthful spirit.

Stepping out of the rental car, peering up, the young woman was all smiles.

"Hope!" said Bud, walking down the steps, his arms out.

"Hello, Dr. Payne."

· · · ·

They embraced near the front steps.

"It's so good to see you, Hope . . . or should I say, Dr. Sapono. And congratulations. First in your class, I understand."

"Thank you." She glanced back at the young man standing behind her. "I want you to meet my husband, Mbato. I wrote you about him. He's a family physician like you."

Mbato quickly offered his hand to Bud. "I'm honored. I've heard much about the Payne family."

"We welcome both of you to the Franklin, Alabama, branch of the Flying Doctors. I'm very honored to have a visiting family physician and a cardiac surgeon share their knowledge with me."

Bud sneaked a glance at Hope's face. For a moment he was afraid he might get emotional. But he stopped himself and asked, "How are the plans for the new clinic going?"

"Great," said Hope enthusiastically. "Except we need everything in the world. I'm going to fill all my pockets with penicillin before we fly back to Nairobi."

"Maybe we should work out a trade. We have lots of penicillin, but not enough doctors who want to practice in rural areas like this."

Mbato said, "It might work. We share rural doctors with you. You share antibiotics with us."

A cloud of dust stirred up as Gail parked a battered pickup truck beside the rental car. Her hair was pulled back in a long ponytail that swung back and forth as she ran toward them.

"Hope . . . dear Hope," she called out, laughing, then wrapping her arms around the young woman. She held out her hand toward Mbato. "It's so nice to meet you. We've heard so many good things."

"You must be exhausted from the flight and the long drive," said Lisa.

Hope spoke for both of them. "Well, as a matter of fact, we could use a few minutes to freshen up."

"Of course," said Gail, glancing at Bud. "We understand, don't we?"

. . . .

"Of course." Bud scanned the sky for incoming aircraft. "We're not expecting any medical emergencies. But, if we get any . . ."

Gail elbowed him in the ribs.

"We'll handle it ourselves," Bud added.

WAIT...THERE'S MORE!

Discover the adventures of real children, like Hope, who come to America from developing countries for heart surgery. Heart to Heart, a non-profit organization, is an international program which has brought children from Africa and South America to the United States for this life-saving surgery. The child, the parent, and the child's doctor journey to American hospitals. The child has surgery, the doctor learns about new programs in medicine, and the Americans learn from and about their guests' culture.

Join the team! Become an honorary member of *The Backyard Tribe* by joining Heart to Heart. Simply fill in the coupon below and mail it in. In turn, you will receive a certificate of membership and a newsletter which will provide you with an opportunity to experience first-hand real stories like *The Backyard Tribe*.

Although *The Backyard Tribe* and characters in the novel are fictional, there is a group of folks from diverse cultures who have joined together and have made stories like these reality.

Application form to become a free
HONORARY MEMBER of The Backyard Tribe
_____ Yes! I want to join Heart to Heart.

Name_____

Address_____

_____ Zip code_____

Phone Number_____

Mail this form or facsimile to:
Heart to Heart
2045 Manchester Street, NE
Atlanta, Georgia 30324
404-875-6263